KEEPER OF THE MOUNTAINS

Other books by Shirlee Smith Matheson

NON-FICTION
Youngblood of the Peace
This Was Our Valley
Flying the Frontiers Vol. I, "A Half Million Hours of Aviation
Adventure"
Flying the Frontiers Vol. II, "More Hours of Aviation Adventure"
Flying the Frontiers Vol. III, "Aviation Adventures Around the World"
A Western Welcome to the World, "A History of Calgary International
Airport"

JUVENILE/YOUNG ADULT FICTION
Prairie Pictures
City Pictures
Flying Ghosts
The Gambler's Daughter

KEEPER OF THE MOUNTAINS

Shirlee Smith Matheson

THISTLEDOWN PRESS

Canadian Cataloguing in Publication Data

Matheson, Shirlee Smith.
Keeper of the Mountains
ISBN 1-894345-13-4
I. Title.
PS8576.A823K44 2000   C813'.54   C00-920063-0
PZ7.M42477Ke 2000

Cover and book design by J. Forrie
Typeset by Thistledown Press Ltd.
Printed and bound in Canada by Veilleux Impression à Demande

Thistledown Press Ltd.
633 Main Street
Saskatoon, Saskatchewan
S7H 0J8

Thistledown Press gratefully acknowledges the financial assistance of the
Canada Council for the Arts, the Saskatchewan Arts Board, and the
Government of Canada through the Book Publishing Industry Development
Program for its publishing program.

ACKNOWLEDGEMENTS

The author wishes to acknowledge assistance from the following organizations and individuals:

Alberta Foundation for the Arts for a grant to facilitate research and writing this book (then titled *Dreams of the Prophets*).

Fort St. John, Fort Nelson and Hudson's Hope museums for provision of archival documents and photographs relating to the Bedaux Sub-Arctic Expedition.

Information gleaned through reading *The Price of Power*, a biography of Charles Eugene Bedaux by Jim Christy (Doubleday Canada Limited, Toronto, 1984), and various newspaper and magazine articles published over the years relating to the expedition. Perusal of diaries and memoirs of several Peace River men hired on the expedition, namely Cecil Pickell, Willard Freer and Bob White.

Material regarding the Two Mountains That Sit Together was gathered from local interviews, Treaty 8 studies relating to the area, and archival documentation.

Special thanks for information and verification of these legendary stories, and the spiritual connotation of the mountains, goes to the late John Dokkie, Beaver (Dunne za) elder and former chief, West Moberly First Nations, and his wife Catherine Dokkie; and to Art Napoleon, community development worker, lifetime resident and former chief, Saulteaux First Nations, Moberly Lake, BC.

CONTENTS

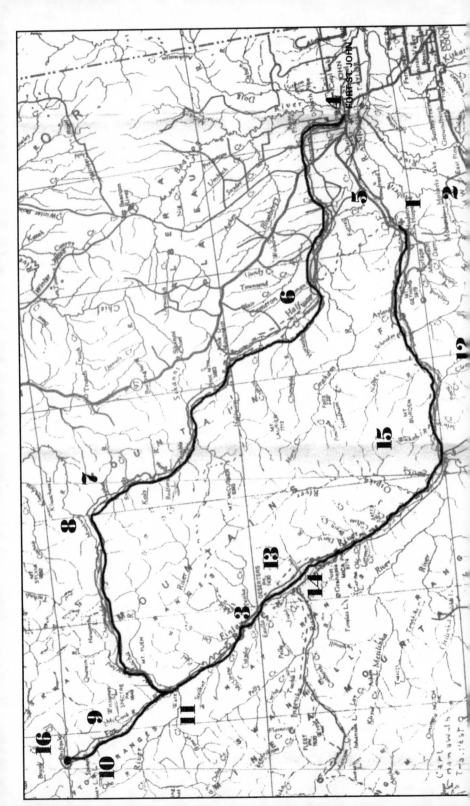

MAP LEGEND

1 Hudson's Hope

2. Moberly Lake

3. Finlay River

4. Fort St. John

5. Peace River

6. Halfway River

7. Prophet River

8. Muskwa River

9. Fox Pass

10. Sifton Pass

11. Fort Ware

12. Clearwater River

13. Deserters Canyon

14. Fort Grahame

15. Wicked River

16. Driftpile River

*To Billy, who turned out to be
a pretty good trail partner*

ONE

THE RICH LOONY

Driving 40 half-wild horses over Rocky Mountain trails didn't give Chris Haldane much spare time to check out the scenery.

He sensed rather than saw the snow-covered peak of Portage Mountain, and to the southwest the sacred Two Mountains That Sit Together. He'd be visiting them soon. Chris had promised his grandmother before she'd died last year that he'd follow the tradition of hiking up to the twin peaks on his fifteenth birthday. That day was coming up next week so he might as well do it on his way home after this wrangling contract was finished. No doubt his mother would give him some sort of a quiz on his findings up there. "What am I supposed to find?" he'd asked. "Spiritual guidance," she'd said mysteriously.

A rider whistled and Chris spurred his horse to catch two renegade cayuses who'd decided to take a side-trip up the Lynx Creek valley. Swinging a coiled lariat, he headed them back onto the trail.

Soon the party had crested the hill above the settlement of Hudson's Hope. Scattered along a plateau overlooking the Peace River were some log cabin homes, a telegraph office, Hudson's Bay trading post, general store and log hotel and café.

"Hey! Yi!" Chris, his trail mates and the horses thundered down the hill toward the holding corrals, spurred on by the thought of the night's hot meal and the fun of meeting up with friends. Tomorrow would come the worst part of the job — swimming the herd across the Peace River — then the relatively easy twenty-mile trek south to Moberly Lake where the buyer was waiting — someone crazy enough to take on 40 horses in October.

The entire Peace River country — the BC part anyway — was Chris' home territory. He'd been born at his parents' trading post called The Forks, where the Finlay and Parsnip rivers collide in the Rocky Mountain Trench to form the mighty Peace. He'd lived there all of his fifteen years, except for his last school term at St. John's in Vancouver.

At first Chris had fought with his parents about going, reminding his father of how he had turned down a chance for higher education and it hadn't hurt him. Chris knew that his father's parents back in Denmark had been rich, and Karl Haldane could have done anything he'd wanted. But, he'd chosen to emigrate to Canada. Not only that, but to the North, where he'd taken over a trading post in the remote mountains.

In the wintertime Karl and Chris ran a trapline up the Clearwater River. In the summer, at the post, they outfitted prospectors. This was pure adventure! Chris loved it as much as his dad did.

His first few months in Vancouver were a nightmare, but he'd survived, made friends and done well at his studies. When he'd returned home in June, he learned there was no money to send him back for a second year.

Chris wheeled his horse around to catch a big buckskin that had spun at the corral gate. His horse expertly blocked the escape and forced the buckskin back. Chris was born to this life, and he knew it, but he'd seen another lifestyle and now felt drawn to that trail, too.

After they'd corralled all the horses and given them water and feed, it was the cowboys' turn. They pitched their gear inside the log bunkhouse, shucked off chaps and spurs, slapped dust from jeans, hung their heads under the water pump, and were really ready for food.

Four dusty wranglers strolling down the main street of Hudson's Hope was nothing to make people take notice, and their only company was an old shaggy brown dog.

Early evening on a warm autumn day in the Peace River country was a magical time. The wide river at this moment was the colour of spun gold. Chris had seen the same water take on hues of the surrounding forests, becoming pale to dark green, or golden like tonight. He'd even seen it turn pink as the evening sun's rays reflected off the snow-capped Rockies to the west. At darkness the water turned coal black but with the rising moon it became a silver ribbon, and a well-lit trail. A good time to travel.

"Everyone gone to bed?" Chris asked, looking around for signs of life.

"Looks like. Maybe we should wake 'em up!" laughed "Hoot" Napoleon, a long-time friend of Chris's. Hoot threw his hat into the air, sending it spiraling upwards. "Yahoo!" He jumped to catch it. Soon all four were flipping their hats, jostling each other, causing dust to puff up from the dirt road.

They were still laughing as they burst into the North Star Café.

Chris surveyed the room. Three tables were occupied, all by people he knew. He nodded greetings. He spotted someone else there too, Billy Turner. Their eyes met, then both looked away as the door from the kitchen swung open and the waitress emerged carrying loaded plates. Chris stopped in his tracks.

She had long blonde hair tied back in a ponytail, and big brown eyes. It was a rare and beautiful combination.

"Jessie!" Chris exclaimed.

She flashed him a quick smile and set down the plates before ducking back into the kitchen. Chris tossed his hat onto the elk-horn rack and took a chair, but not before he caught the look on Billy Turner's face.

In the bush country, you have to be ready for every kind of cross-up. But Chris had never expected to see Jessie Watson serving food to range-rough cowboys in the North Star Café. He now tried to concentrate on steaks and chops sizzling on the grill, huge kettles of mashed potatoes and steamed vegetables, and fresh buns piled like cannonballs along the counter, barely leaving room for the pies.

As he sat down he heard the cowboys laughing at the back table.

"Aw, shaddap you buncha ignoramuses," interrupted an older voice. "Save your breath to cool your soup."

Recognizing the voice, Chris and Hoot turned to see some friends at a table in the back of the room. "Skid" Desjarlais was sitting with the old prospector, Einar Olson. Good. Chris and Hoot gave a "see-ya" wave to their trail partners, and joined them.

14

Skid, named from the way he stops his horse, and Hoot, who could mimic the call of any wild bird, were both from Moberly Lake, twenty miles to the south of Hudson's Hope. The Desjarlais and Napoleon families lived on the Cree/Saulteaux reserve at the east end of Moberly Lake. Skid's grandfather, William, had signed onto Treaty 8 for that reserve.

Chris's mother was from the Dunne-Za tribe (called "Castor" in French and "Beaver" in English). Although her people had lived on the Halfway River, a Beaver reserve had been established at the west end of Moberly Lake. These families often met with the Cree and Saulteaux at common hunting and berry-picking areas, including the mysterious Two Mountains that Sit Together, and the boys had known each other from childhood.

Skid was tall and lanky, slow-spoken, with a good sense of humour. Hoot was a bit stockier, strong as a horse, with a happy-go-lucky personality. Both were excellent bushmen, and could survive any winter with just a gun and a sack of salt.

Chris had known Einar Olson for many years. The old fellow washed gold on Pete Toy's Bar up the Finlay River and bought his supplies at The Forks.

"Hey, you guys responsible for bringing those mangy broom-tails into town?" asked Skid, smiling.

Chris and Hoot nodded.

"Who you fixing to sell them to?"

"Someone named Bedaux is paying top dollar," Chris said. "They're good stock. Hand-picked."

The guys laughed.

Chris heard the waitress coming toward their table and held out his coffee cup. "Yowch!" He jumped as a few drops of hot coffee spilled onto his hand.

"Sorry," Jessie said nervously.

"Didn't expect to see you here," Chris said as nonchalantly as possible.

"You either," was her reply.

"So, why're you here?"

"Same reason you are!" she shot back. "Earning a living." She turned, wielding the pot like a sword.

Chris had known Jessie ever since her folks had come into the country to ranch on the lower Halfway River. It was from her father, Albert Watson, that Jessie had inherited her blonde hair, and from her mother, Bernice, her snapping dark eyes.

"This is my last day in town for the season," Skid said, breaking the silence. "I'm heading out to the trapline tomorrow."

"Big dance tonight," added Einar. "Who's playing, Jessie?" he called out.

"Matt and Andy Brewer."

"Good," said Hoot. "We'd better go, eh Chris? You could ask Jessie."

"Oh yeah, sure. She won't even serve me!" He looked over at their two wrangling partners who were already chowing down. He avoided looking over at Billy Turner's table, just heard their chairs scrape back as they got up to leave.

"Tell you what you do," old Einar said, in a voice that carried across the room. "Tell Jessie you're sorry for something. Don't matter what, make it up. Then you ask, real nice like, for some of that good food. When you're on your second piece of pie, ask her if she made it 'cause it's almost as good as your ma's. Then — ask her to the dance."

Chris was embarrassed at receiving advice in a public place, but Billy had already left, thankfully.

"Hey, Einar!" Hoot said, "you know so much about women, how come you're not married?"

"That's why I ain't," said Einar. "Women like to order you around — make you wash up after a day's work when you're plumb tired. Shave for no reason. Wear your good pants on Sunday even when you aren't going nowhere. Make you stop cussing. Tell you don't smoke your pipe in the house. Won't let the dog in . . ."

When Jessie again approached the table, Chris was in a lighter mood. "I'd like a steak, medium rare, with the works, please," he said with a smile. She smiled back.

The conversation then went to horses, and to work that paid cash money.

"Some crazy Frenchman is coming up here, bringing motor cars to Fort St. John. Then they plan to travel through the bush, straight to the Pacific Ocean!" Skid announced.

"There's no road!" Chris said. "No bridges! Not even a game trail."

"We know that! So, he's crazy, but he's paying good money, four bucks a day, for packers and trail breakers. Why not apply, Chris? I did."

The food arrived. Chris and Hoot dug in.

"Bedaux's buying horses and hiring cowboys to go 600 miles through the bush, cutting trail and packing supplies — food, gas for the cars, everything," Skid said.

"That's the guy whose buying these horses we're driving! Why would he be buying horses and hiring

17

packers if he's using motor cars?" Chris asked. "Is he some kind of a rich loony?"

"What's a car?" was old Einar's question.

"Cars are rubber-tired buggies driven by gasoline engines instead of horses," Skid explained. "They're Citröens, made in France, with special tracks to go over rough land. Bedaux drove them across the Sahara Desert back in '29. Nearly ten thousand miles!"

"Maybe so," Einar said, "but deserts is flat. There's no cliffs or mountains or river rapids to cross in deserts. What does he know about this country?"

"He checked things out here a couple of years ago and he said he was coming back. So, he's coming next spring."

"He thought a road could be built from Fort St. John west through the mountains to the Pacific coast!" Skid added. "Crazy! No way you could get through those passes in winter."

Einar Olson shook his finger in the air for attention. "What do we need a road for? Horses, boats or snowshoes get me anywhere I need to go. And if I can't get through, I figure it's none of my business what's on the other side of them mountains or rivers."

Everyone laughed, but knew Einar had a point.

Jessie came over to remove Chris's empty plate. "Could I have some of that great-looking pie?" Chris asked.

Jessie smiled. "Apple or pumpkin?"

"Take the pumpkin!" Einar whispered hoarsely, and nodded toward Jessie meaning "that's the one she made."

"Pumpkin," Chris said, "à la mode!"

A man at the neighbouring table leaned back, exhaled a cloud of smoke, and said, "Bedaux's doing this for only one reason — it hasn't been done."

Einar laughed. "Nobody's fell off Portage Mountain neither. Maybe he should try that."

"This Bedaux guy is either a genius or completely nuts," Chris decided. "Or, there could be something behind his plan, something none of us has even thought about."

"Maybe all those things," agreed Hoot. "But I don't care. Where can I get hold of him to sign up?"

"I've got his letter in my pack," Skid said. "You write him too, Chris! From what I hear, with all this crazy stuff he's bringing up it's gonna be some wild trail ride."

"I just might do that," Chris smiled. He said "So-long" to his friends and old Einar, and grabbed his hat off the rack. The cowhands had already left. Chris started toward the door, then hesitated. Taking a deep breath, he wheeled around and pushed through the swinging doors of the kitchen.

TWO

THE DANCE

Chris and Jessie could hear the pounding beat of the music before they arrived at the dance hall. Hudson's Hope people were always ready for a party, and any excuse would do.

Chris helped Jessie with her coat, and hung it on a peg while she started chatting to some neighbours from the Halfway River. Chris noticed some of his friends, trappers and prospectors, and went over to get the latest news. He'd ask Jessie to dance after everyone had loosened up a bit.

Old Billy Mahaffy, a miner from up the Finlay River near Ingenika, told Chris about the new interest in the country by big mining companies. "Six riverboats full of engineers and geologists been up and down the Omineca, Ospika, and Ingenika rivers in the past month alone!" he said excitedly. "Don't know what they're doing, but I don't like all these strangers around. Bad for animals. Bad for people."

"But it's good for trade," Chris objected.

"Hah! They bring in their own supplies, bought cheaper down south. Just leave their junk here, empty fuel barrels, all their crap and corruption." The miner shook his finger at Chris, and his eyes took on a steely glint. "Let me tell you, son, this country can only support so many human beings. This so called Sub-Arctic Expedition sounds like a hootin' good time and it'll bring in some quick bucks for locals, but the Bedaux's of the world don't do nothing for nothing."

Chris was about to admit that he was thinking of signing up himself when he saw Jessie whirling around the floor — in the arms of Billy Turner! Of all guys, why did she have to dance with him?

Chris had little respect for Billy Turner, after having a few run-ins with him. Billy was a kid who'd been brought up to fight. Old man Turner was a bull of a man, one of the toughest of the old-time teamsters that had come up to the Peace from the Cariboo area. Anyone who could drive those big mule teams and sit a buckboard all day, and make enough at it to pay off a ranch, had to be strong. He'd fought for everything he had, and raised his son to follow the same method.

Last summer Billy and Chris had worked on the Silvertip Ranch just above the Peace Canyon. Chris had tolerated Billy's bullying ways to avoid trouble, but when he saw Billy knocking around the horses he couldn't keep silent. It wasn't his style to rat to the foreman, so he'd confronted Billy directly. Billy's reply was a punch in the guts that took Chris' wind. The battle was on.

Chris had taken some boxing training at school, and he needed it as Billy had him for size and belligerence. A stiff right to Billy's nose caused a shower of blood, and at the sight of his own blood Billy turned pale and nearly passed out. He wanted no more.

They'd washed up in the creek and mentioned the affair to no one. The horses appreciated Billy's attitude adjustment.

Now, Chris felt a sudden need for some fresh air. Even in the darkness he could see the men gathered down by a clump of spruce trees, and a jug being passed among some of them. As he strolled toward the group, Billy Turner came out of the hall and swaggered down the steps.

"We got some business, Haldane," he said loudly. It was obvious he hadn't missed any turns at the jug.

"Well, if it ain't Charmin' Billy — you want to ask me to dance?"

Billy's fist shot out and grazed the side of Chris' head. His automatic reaction was a right uppercut to Billy's jaw and a left jab that set him spinning. On his turnaround, Billy swung wildly and caught Chris on the lower jaw. Chris was on the ground. The lights from the hall seemed to spin, making the tall dark building resemble a merry-go-round. Just the stars were for real.

Skid and Hoot were at Chris's side, fists up, ready to lay out Billy or anyone else who had the same notion. No one did. They grabbed his arms and legs, and carried him under a tree where nobody would step on him. When Chris sat up, Billy and his friends were nowhere to be seen.

"You'll be all right in a minute," Hoot said. "Just put an ice pack on that jawbone."

Then Chris saw Jessie. She stood on the steps, silhouetted in the light from the hall. She walked down the steps and came over to the tree, kneeling down beside Chris.

"I'm sorry," she said.

"What for?"

"It's my fault," she whispered.

"Let's go inside. You can tell me about it while we dance." Chris struggled to his feet, amazed at how great he suddenly felt.

"Billy asked to take me home tonight," Jessie said. "I told him I was going home with you."

"You told him right!" Chris began moving to the music, but his mind was leaping like a trout up a waterfall. Billy Turner had a way of getting even.

When the music stopped and midnight supper was served, everyone started talking about Bedaux — French genius or rich loony?

Billy Turner reentered the hall just as supper was ending and the band was picking up again.

"Let's go," Jessie whispered.

Chris agreed, and was getting her coat when Billy approached. His blackening eye and swollen jaw didn't hurt his looks much, or help his temperament.

"You'd better watch it, Haldane," Billy muttered as he pushed past.

Jessie came walking up at that moment and Billy looked over at her. He started to say something, then turned on his heel, leapt down the steps of the dance hall, and disappeared into the night.

"What did he say to you?" Jessie asked anxiously.

"Oh, nothing. He was just letting off some steam."

"I've known him ever since we moved out to the ranch. He and his dad have one of the best ranches in the Halfway area. You always see them working, from sunup to sundown. Mrs. Turner died last spring and since then they've lived like cavemen. You'd better be careful."

"I didn't know about that," Chris said. "I worked all summer with Billy on the Silvertip Ranch. Didn't like him, mean as a snake with the horses."

"Yeah. I've seen all sides of Billy, but the good side hasn't shown up much lately. Mom and Dad invite them over for supper every so often. Sometimes they come, sometimes they don't. He should get away for a while, but says he doesn't like to leave his father."

The nights were getting cold this late in the year, and above the banks of the Peace River the Northern Lights flickered and danced. Jessie walked close beside him, and it seemed only natural to drape his arm around her shoulders.

"I've been trying to recall where I first heard of your family," Chris said. "I remember your dad stopping at our trading post once on his way upriver to Prince George. He was bringing back some new farm machinery. He's from England, isn't he?"

"My father was an officer in the British Army," she replied. "He made the mistake of falling in love with the wrong person."

"Hey, I don't mean to pry!"

"No, it's okay. Mom was an actress, and Irish. My father's family didn't think much of theatre people, or the Irish. They got married and came to Canada. Father had heard of the rich Peace River country — and we've been here for almost eight years now."

They walked on without talking. At the back of Chris's mind was Billy Turner and his surprising attack. Then he started thinking about the Bedaux job. And the question he had to resolve about going back to school. It would be good to get away for awhile, for more reasons than one.

"What are you thinking about?" Jessie asked.

"Work," he said.

"Men!" She gave a little laugh, quickly kissed him on the cheek and ducked inside the house, closing the door quietly so she wouldn't wake up the people with whom she boarded.

Hey! She strikes quicker than Billy Turner! And more accurately.

The whole day had been so haywire that Chris could hardly keep from laughing out loud. The hurt in his jaw felt good.

He'd send a letter to the Bedaux outfit. It would be a great experience. But now he had to get ready for tomorrow's task, a crack-of-dawn swim across the near-freezing Peace River with 40 loose broncs.

THREE
THE TWIN MOUNTAINS

Chris woke at dawn to the chorus of three snoring cowboys, 40 snorting horses, and a squawky magpie.

After they'd lightly fed the horses, it was time to feed themselves — but not so lightly.

Chris never expected the sudden fame that greeted him when he walked into the café. "Hey, Haldane, you a lover or a fighter?" one of the cowboys shouted. He felt his face flush, nearly as red as Jessie's when she brought the breakfast plates to their table. But she looked great with her gold-blonde hair tied up in a blue ribbon.

Before he'd finished eating, Chris heard from three different people that Billy Turner had left town uttering a warning: "I'll get even with Haldane." Fine. If Bully Billy wanted tough, he'd get it.

"Let's go!" the trail boss called. Chris stood up and reached for his hat, and Jessie quickly shoved a paper bag into his hand. He could only mumble, "Thank you," before he scooted, hearing laughter follow him out the door.

He could smell the contents of the bag and guess what it contained even before he opened it. Fresh doughnuts!

Nearly two dozen! Although he'd just eaten a big meal, he wolfed down six before he reached the corral.

The horses were frisky and that was good. They'd need lots of energy. Chris saddled up his mare, and stowed the doughnuts.

"A man should have no trouble handling a tough job if he has a sack of doughnuts in his saddlebag and a pretty girl on his mind," commented one of the cowboys. Chris spurred his horse and went after a stray, glad to escape.

But the mare had her own plan to start the day. Chris had been taught by the old cowhands that the best relationships between men and horses were where each had something over the other. The "something" he had over this little spitfire was that he was better at sticking to her than she was at bucking him off. The "something" she had was knowing when the contest would be. This morning was one of those times.

At the touch of the spur, the mare corkscrewed straight up and the world blurred. Chris hung on tight as she bucked down the trail. Then, she settled down as quickly as she'd started up. "Good morning, hoss!" Chris laughed to himself.

They headed to the crossing, where a river-man was waiting with a boat. They threw in the saddles and equipment and Chris climbed in, taking the rope of the lead mare. The cowboys whooped and waved their hats as they chased the ponies into the river.

At the shock of the ice-cold water the mare's backbone stiffened like a beam. She snorted and tried to rear back, but Chris held firm and urged her along. He could hear the yells of the cowboys on the north shore, making sure the horses didn't swing back.

All 40 horses, plus their saddlehorses, clambered onto the gravel bar on the south shore, shaking off enough water to start a garden. The boat returned for the cowboys, and then they had the work of saddling up before hitting the trail to Moberly Lake.

The ride to their delivery point, the Beaver Indian settlement on the west end of the lake, was the most pleasant part of the trip for Chris. To the west the snow-peaks of the Two Mountains That Sit Together glimmered in the autumn sunlight. These mountains held a magic that was hard to explain.

"The twin mountains are the hunting territory of the Dunne-Za, the Beaver Indians," his grandmother had explained. "We are the original custodians."

People from Moberly Lake and also from the Halfway River traditionally came to seek *mayine*, a supernatural power from animals, which could only be gained through a stay on these sacred slopes.

Chris's grandmother said that at one time the Beaver and Sikanni — People of the Rocks — were once the same tribe and shared the Athapaskan language base common to all Dene tribes, but they'd split up. The Sikannis now lived on the mountains, and along the Finlay and Parsnip rivers and tributaries, while the Beaver dwelt in the Peace River valleys of British Columbia and Alberta. Only those who knew their languages well could point out the differences.

The Cree from the east side of Moberly Lake called these twin peaks *Kanesostegaw Asineewachia*, and reached them by way of the old Beaver Indian trail to Carbon Creek.

Chris knew about the mountains because of the legends he'd been told so often by his grandmother, Agathe

Deschene. Chris was born October 16, 1918, during an early fall hunting trip when his mother and father were travelling with her family, the Deschenes, to the Two Mountains That Sit Together. In the moments following his birth, his grandmother had held him up facing the rising sun, and sung a secret song to connect his spirit forever to the mountains.

When Chris was six years old, his grandmother had come to live with them. Before she died a year ago, the year Chris turned fourteen, she had taught him the natural ways of life and of the old teachings. "Be proud of your mixed blood," she'd said. "It will give you an advantage over others, who know only one way to see things."

He had grown up like any boy in that country, learning how to survive in the bush, and to cherish the land. He'd learned enough to get by in the languages of the trading post's customers: English and French, the Algonquian dialects of Cree — the major communion used in the fur trade — and Saulteaux, and even the difficult Athapaskan dialects of Beaver and Sikanni.

"You have some Indian blood, French, Danish, and probably a mixture of a few other nations, so that makes you pure Canadian!" his father had said, after Chris was teased about the odd combination of his light blue eyes, black hair and olive skin.

As Chris followed the herd of horses along the trail to Moberly Lake, he decided that when this job was finished he'd visit at Moberly Lake, then head home across country toward the mountains. He looked forward to staying a night or two in the wilderness. It would give him time to think and clear his head.

They delivered the horses in good shape, and each collected his twenty dollars cash. The stock broker had provided the cowboys with saddles, stock and gear to make this ride, and would be picking them up again in a week or so. Chris gave the spunky little mare a farewell slap on the rump, and shook hands goodbye with his three partners who were heading through Jackfish Lake to Dawson Creek before that cash burned holes in their jeans.

Chris packed his riding boots, pulled on his trail moccasins, and started the 90-mile trek home. After so many days in the saddle, it felt good to be on his feet. He planned to go up the Moberly River, follow the Carbon to the Peace, and catch a ride the rest of the way home with King Gething on his last mail run up the river on October 12th.

Near Johnson Creek he came upon a Beaver Indian hunting camp. There were ten teepees housing three extended families. A group of women and children were busy slicing meat, scraping moose hides, chopping bones, and tending fires under drying racks. A few young boys were gathering and chopping wood, while other children strung meat on racks and kept the fires smoking. The men had killed six moose. Now they were standing at the edge of the camp, smoking, feeling good about their fall hunt.

He talked with the men, who told him it was a good year for moose and caribou. Behind the twin mountains they'd also seen mountain sheep, grizzly and black bear. He couldn't help but notice how hard the women worked. He'd often seen groups of women and kids, walking along single-file as if in a pack-string, carrying home the meat from a big hunt like this. It was fairly common to see old grandmothers packing a front quarter or a moose head.

After trading a pouch of tobacco for some dried moose meat, called *Kakiyak* in Cree, he continued on.

It took a day to climb one of the twin peaks, and he could see for miles in all directions. He made a small fire and cut some spruce boughs for a bed. When night fell and the moon came up, the ridges of the Rockies resembled the points of an old fort. There was a skiff of snow on the ground, and he knew more would come soon. In this country you get short warning: you see some snow come, and soon you're standing in it.

Chris spent a cold night lying beside his small fire, turning to warm his back, then his front. Soon the low flames became red embers, glowing and dying, then gathering life momentarily when a breeze whipped past. Perhaps it was his imagination but Chris could see pictures in the fire's bed — a face, a cross, an arrow, crossed arrows. Wolf howls echoed from valley to valley below, accented by hooty calls of owls.

Dawn broke slowly, and the rays of light arced across the peaks, turning cold silver to warm gold, pink, orange, to be replaced finally by bright blue.

Chris chewed on some dried meat while he boiled up a pot of coffee.

His downward path brought him to an old gravesite, piled high with rocks. His grandmother had instructed him to carry a coloured cloth — yellow, red, white or blue — called a Prayer Flag in English or *Weepinasona* in Cree, to offer with tobacco, to open the spiritual pathways. Kneeling, he said a silent prayer.

He slept the next night again without shelter, keeping a small fire going. But he slept fitfully, and when he awoke he held the memory of a vivid dream: he would live to see a mighty river die. The vision was so clear. He'd been standing on the very top of this mountain, looking down. The world below was covered with water, but no rivers ran.

Was this a dream or a nightmare? Maybe it was punishment, he thought, because he hadn't stopped long enough at the graves, or observed the proper rituals of walking around the site four times, singing the prayer song, or refrained from eating. He hadn't slept in the correct position away from the trail with his head toward the rising sun. His mind had been too alive with questions, too crowded by silly things — an attraction to a golden-haired, brown-eyed, girl, a stupid fight that wasn't over yet, and a desire to join an oddball expedition that would pay him more money in six months than he usually made from six seasons' work.

Chris felt strange being here now, and was anxious to leave the Two Mountains That Sit Together. But he knew he would return, and the next time he visited this sacred site he would bring more worthy thoughts.

As he descended, a backward glance left him with an eerie feeling as if eyes were trained on him. Then he dropped down to Carbon Creek and followed it to the Peace. Right on time, he heard the chug! chug! of King Gething's engine and saw his riverboat coming around the bend.

October 25, 1933
Dear Mr. Bedaux:
I heard of your expedition starting next spring from my friend, Skid Desjarlais, who you've hired to wrangle horses.

*Our crew just brought in 40 horses you bought. I have
worked on ranches and know the areas you plan to
travel.*
*Please consider me for your expedition as I'm a good
wrangler.*
Yours truly,
Chris Haldane

The following month Chris received word that he was one
of some 50 men chosen to be part of Charles Bedaux's
Sub-Arctic Expedition.

In December, Chris and Karl Haldane travelled by dog
team to Hudson's Hope for supplies. After loading up,
Chris stepped into the North Star Café. Billy Turner was
sitting backwards on a chair, working a toothpick.

"Congratulations, Haldane, hear you got hired on. It
must have been the good word I put in for you."

"If you were any help to me, Billy boy, it would be the
first time."

Jessie poured his coffee and refilled Billy's as Karl
Haldane entered the café. It was rare to see Karl in town,
and many were eager to hear news of The Forks.

As Billy left the café, he muttered in a low voice as he
passed Chris. "I'm glad you're coming along, Haldane.
Wouldn't do to have you hanging around town all summer,
bothering my girl."

The heat rose in Chris, but then he noticed all eyes in
the café were on him, including his father's, and he let it
pass. The coffee burned his throat as he gulped down the
remainder in his cup and hurried outside to cool off.

FOUR
HORSES, MEN AND A MULE

In Hudson's Hope that spring of 1934 everyone was talking about Charles Bedaux. Because he'd hired many local people, the entire Peace River country became involved in the northern safari.

The Bedaux party planned to travel in high style. The cowboys would be looking after more than 100 horses — packing and unpacking panniers and grub-boxes filled with supplies to outfit a moving camp of about 50 people.

The first duty was to attend the send-off party. Chris planned to dance with every woman in the place, but when Jessie came in he just couldn't see anyone else.

Walking home after the dance, they stopped to watch the moon rise over the dark canopy of trees across the river.

"I'll be gone 'til fall," Chris said. "I guess I'll see you then."

"I wish I could meet those rich people," Jessie replied. "What a great adventure you'll have!"

"I'll write and I'll report every detail, even the ladies' hair and clothes styles, if you want!"

She laughed, and he laughed too. He felt great.

"Billy Turner left three weeks ago to ride with the Trail-Cutters Party. I've promised to write to him, too," Jessie said.

"Why?"

"He asked me to give him news about his father and the ranch. Lyle Turner isn't the letter-writing type, so I'll be — "

"—Billy's faithful pen pal." Chris had to laugh. That Billy was dumb like a fox.

Jessie smiled, and Chris put his arm around her as they continued to walk. "I want to become a teacher," she said. "I took my first three years of schooling in Ontario, then when we moved here I had to do it by correspondence. I always thought it would be wonderful to be in a real school again! Now I am, and I want to teach."

"You'd make a good teacher. The students would all be in love with you," Chris said.

"Well, I'd be in love with them, too," Jessie responded. "Going to school here in Hudson's Hope is such fun. I help the teacher, Miss Edwards, by giving reading and arithmetic lessons to the little ones."

"I admire what you're doing. It can't be easy, attending classes, working in the café, and trying to study."

"You did it, too," she said. "You must have taken school by correspondence and then helped out at The Forks."

"Oh yeah. I took the first nine years by correspondence, and then I was sent to boarding school in Vancouver."

"So I heard," she said. "Lucky you. It must be wonderful to live in Vancouver."

Chris grinned at her. "I'd rather be here any day. In fact, that's why I didn't go back in September. I decided I liked it here better."

He wouldn't tell her how much he wanted to return but just couldn't afford it. Now, being hired by Bedaux, he'd be able to pay his own way and return next fall. Missing a year wasn't a major tragedy and it would be an exciting, fun-filled year.

"You're crazy," she said. "If I had your chance to attend school in the city, I'd be gone in a minute."

Chris felt his face grow warm in the cool night air. "I thought you loved this country, too," he said.

"I do. That's why I want to get an education, so I can come back and teach. There is no school at the Halfway River and there are lots of homesteading families with kids."

"You're planning on coming back here, to the Halfway?" Chris asked incredulously.

"Why not? You should consider doing the same, Chris. Finish high school, get your university degree, do something here."

That night in the bunkhouse, Chris tossed and turned on his slab-board bunk. Finally, he took his bedroll and laid it out beneath a big spruce tree. He fell into a deep sleep just as the magpie began its bugle practice.

For the 60-mile journey down the Peace River to Fort St. John, Chris, Skid, Hoot, and an older cowboy named Smoky Sloan built a raft. They cut a pair of jackpines and tied the poles together with their saddle ropes. After breakfast, Jessie brought out a sack of fresh cinnamon buns. "I'll be at the landing to see you off," she whispered as she handed Chris the bag.

It was late in the morning of Sunday, June 24th, when they were finally ready to leave from the ferry landing below the town. The citizens of Hudson's Hope were there to see them off — most of whom hadn't yet made it to bed. The raft was piled with bedrolls, changes of clothes, and riding gear — saddles, spurs and chaps.

Chris looked at Jessie standing in the crowd. Should he, or shouldn't he? Why not? He strode toward her. "Wanna meet the Bedaux?" He lifted her high into the air and set her on the raft. Amidst her squeals and the laughter of the crowd, he helped her back onto the dock and kissed her good-bye. Then he gave the raft a push-off and leapt on as the current caught it and swung it downstream. He could see her waving a blue scarf until the raft went around the bend of the river.

Sunlight sparkled on the twisting ropes of olive green water, making it hard to see without squinting. They spotted a number of moose along the riverbanks. At their approach, a black bear with cubs scrambled up the gravel bar and into the trees. Chris loved river travel — reading the water's flow, navigating riffles and rapids, searching out deep channels, steering around eddies or sandbars.

Seven miles downstream they passed through a high formation of rock known as The Gates. Deciding on the best channel was tricky, but the crew knew this river.

Their raft floated past Cache Creek and soon arrived at the mouth of the Moberly River. It was now ten o'clock at night, but it seemed earlier because in the Peace country the sun hangs in the sky until late.

"It's time we camped," Smoky said. "We'll stiffen up if we sit too long on this raft. Air gets damp when the sun goes down."

They noticed an old cabin and pulled in. After a supper of bacon and bannock they spread out their bedrolls on the ground — leaving the cabin to the pack rats — and slept until daybreak.

To speed up their progress for the last ten miles they rigged a tarp sail, and arrived at the ferry landing at Fort St. John by mid-morning. They unloaded their gear, pulled the raft to shore, untied their ropes, then hiked up the steep hill to the town-site four miles to the north.

Their orders were to contact a fellow by the name of Edward Mayo.

"I met Mr. Mayo once," Chris said to his companions. "He came in to buy supplies at The Forks. He's weird!"

"No kidding," Skid said. "I met him on the trail, middle of winter. He runs the snarliest team of Alsatian Huskies in the country — named after the Apostles, no less. He was running behind those dogs wearing mukluks and an army shirt and shorts! Knobby old knees sticking out, shirt open, no underwear. And a red bandanna around his head!"

"Everyone knows about those dogs, and him," Hoot added. "And now he's our boss. Yikes!"

"He's got a place up on the Wicked River, across the Peace River from Finlay Bay." Chris said. "Comes to The Forks with his furs."

Smoky Sloan had listened to the discussion. "I know 'Nick' Mayo fairly well," he drawled, as he rolled a smoke. "His name's Edward but he goes by Nick. You'll be calling him Mister, or Commander." Smoky stopped to strike a match against his pant leg and lit his hand-rolled smoke.

"Tell us about him!" Chris urged. "What's his game? Why does he dress like that? Where did he come from?"

"He's a neighbour of mine, has a cabin up on the Wicked River as you know. Does some trapping, but

mostly prospects for gold along the Peace and the Finlay."
Smoky's grey eyes squinted through the smoke from his
cigarette. "British Royal Navy man. Tough as leather."

—❈—

As Commander Mayo inspected his crew, it was hard to
know if he approved or disapproved. The boys checked
him out at the same time. Mayo was tall, lean, wiry, and
energetic. He was dressed in a khaki shirt and shorts, wool
socks and hiking boots. He wore a black silk bandanna
around his head, and his long greying brown hair flowed
beneath it. His sharp blue eyes missed nothing.

"Welcome, men, to the Bedaux Sub-Arctic Expedition!"
Mayo said in a strong British accent. "It will be an adven-
ture you won't soon forget." Suddenly he was all business.
"We're making a temporary camp on Fish Creek north of
Fort St. John. From this base we'll pick about 60 horses
for their training, strength, and personalities."

Among the horses was a female mule, purchased on
Mayo's orders. "She'll be my mount for the trip," he
announced, to the cowboys' amazement.

"No surprise Nick and the mule took a shine to each
other," Hoot commented with a grin. "They're both pecu-
liar."

Mules weren't too common in the country, but the
Silvertip Ranch had a couple and Chris liked them because
they were smarter than horses. Only problem was, it was
thought their small hooves would sink in spongy muskeg.
"It's crazy to take that mule on this trip," he said to Smoky.
"We've got miles of muskeg ahead in the Muskwa River
country."

Commander Mayo disgustedly watched the horses play their silly games. "We wouldn't be having trouble with finicky animals if we packed all mules," he muttered.

"But if even one horse runs away, a mule will follow it," said Skid, a true horseman. "They've got no sense of independence."

But even Skid had his hands full as he attempted to teach etiquette to a big chestnut gelding that weighed around 1,200 pounds. He was supposed to be broke, but he'd buck, kick, snort and throw himself around whenever he felt like it.

"I'm going to call this one 'Dog Meat'!" Skid yelled as the horse once again threw him to the ground.

Chris laughed. "I'd call him 'Boss' if I were you!"

The horses were to be shod before leaving on the trip, the packhorses just on their front feet but the saddle horses all around. A pile of Riley-McCormick pack saddles had been shipped in from Calgary, as well as some hand-made saddles for the bigger horses, and a few army packsaddles. When Mayo became concerned about the lack of horse blankets, Chris spoke up.

"How about using some of this bedding that's been shipped up for the Dudes?" He indicated the mountain of supplies. "There's more here than they'll need. Could we open up a pack and use it on the horses?"

"Splendid idea!" Mayo agreed.

"These animals aren't going to be unpacked at noon stopovers. They've got to have good padding to carry packs all day," Mayo said when questioned by the warehouseman about borrowing from the Dudes' supplies. And so the packhorses sported pink and blue blankets, complete with satin trim.

The Advance Party, which had the job of transporting gasoline in twenty-gallon tanks to be left at ten-mile intervals for the Citröen vehicles, included 50 packhorses, seven saddle-horses, one mule, and eight men, including Commander Mayo. The men were all from the Peace country and knew each other. Chris, Skid and Hoot were called the "kids" by the older cowboys. Their cook was a big, burly man from Moberly Lake named Wilson Baker. His nickname was Amoo, which means "Bumblebee" in Cree, because of his legendary fear of, and allergy to, the stingers.

The Trail-Cutters Party had already started out. Tommy Wilde, a local cowboy, was their leader — a combination cook and party chief. Tommy knew the trail to the coast, having travelled before from Fort St. John to Telegraph Creek.

The Trail-Cutters job was to slash a navigable six-foot wide trail through the bush for the Citröens using axes and Swede saws, and leaving stumps not more than six inches high. With them was a land surveyor and nine cowboys, including Billy Turner.

FIVE
TRAIL BLAZES

E ach cowboy picked his own saddlehorse for the trip. The one that appealed to Chris was a big black gelding with a white slash down his forehead. He looked as if he'd dipped his nose into a bucket of whitewash and then tossed his head back. The horse's eyes showed humour, and his back was straight and strong, with good-sized hindquarters for the rough trails ahead. Chris named him Flash.

The packhorses were a mixture of mares and geldings, but they were to be kept apart from the saddlehorses, "so there would be no social problems," as Smoky Sloan put it. Chris spotted his little mare in the pack. He named her Babe and decided she'd be his second mount if Flash needed time off. In the meantime, she'd double as a pack-horse.

Most of the men gave names to their saddlehorses, but Smoky refused. "Why name something you might have to eat?" was his philosophy.

Smoky's comment made Chris think about what they were getting into, and he couldn't shake a feeling of fore-boding. They were entering wild country, but not without some protection. Mayo carried a .303 British rifle, Smoky was an ace shot, Hoot had a .22, and Skid and Chris each packed 30-30 Winchester carbines.

But travelling in the wild country, especially at high altitudes where the soil was rocky and there wasn't much feed, or across rivers and through miles of muskeg, was going to be hard on the horses.

Morning began at dawn as it took several hours to wrangle and rig 57 horses and the mule. These animals weren't used to carrying packs and some jumped around in an attempt to pitch them off. Others refused to follow in a line and wandered off through the trees, or raced ahead to be in the lead. The cowboys rode back and forth along the pack-line, moving them along the trail through the narrow grade to Fish Creek. The first day they travelled just twelve miles.

Commander Mayo sometimes rode, but often led, his Molly-mule. Dressed, as usual, in army shorts, a heavy cotton drill shirt with sleeves rolled above his elbows and the silk bandanna tied around his head, he resembled a pirate. His .303 rifle was stuck under the stirrup leather to the left of his saddle, his trail ax on the right, and a two-foot long machete suspended down the front. A couple of wool coats were rolled up and tied behind his saddle, along with a hat that he never wore. Molly looked just as strange, outfitted with Mayo's English-style bridle and saddle.

Mayo was also accompanied by a little black mutt named Rubbish that he'd picked up as a stray in Fort St. John. "No one is to feed this dog," Mayo announced. "He has to pay his own way, catch his own food, rabbits, mice, whatever he can find along the trail." The little dog looked up and wagged his tail. His owner leaned down and gave him one quick pet on the head, a high-point of emotion for Commander Mayo.

"Day One was a good test," Mayo announced as they prepared camp. "Chris and Hoot have night watch."

The two young cowboys looked at each other, then at the herd of jumpy animals. "Oh, great," Chris commented. "None of these animals has been together before. Count on some action while they settle the pecking order."

Hoot agreed. "We can herd them into that bend in the riverbank. They won't wander. There's good grass."

"I'd say hobble and tie bells on a couple of them," Mayo suggested.

When he had ridden off, Chris and Hoot looked at the horses — standing, heads down, munching grass. "They won't wander off," Hoot repeated. "They're tired, like us. They just want to eat and sleep."

"Aw, better do what he says," Chris said.

Hoot grinned. "Flip a coin. Heads we leave 'em off, tails we bell and hobble a few like the boss-man says."

"Deal," Chris said. "But if they get away . . . "

"Then I'll owe you one."

Hoot brought out a quarter from his pocket. The silver coin flipped into the air; he caught it and slapped it onto the back of his hand. Both stared down.

"Heads," Chris said. "Oh, boy." The horses would not be hobbled.

They made a small fire and lay on their bedrolls, talking to keep awake, looking at the stars, pointing out the few they knew by name. They laughed as an owl made a low sound. Hoot answered back and the owl responded. "You're the only guy I know who can carry on a conversation with an owl," Chris said.

"Pretty smart owl," Hoot said. "Tells me that the horses are behaving themselves out there."

They could hear the horses grazing down in the clearing, emitting the occasional contented snort, as well as a few screeches as bites or kicks were exchanged. Normal.

Hours later, Chris sat up, straining to hear in the darkness. Nothing. Absolute silence. Hoot, too, had fallen asleep. Chris got up and made his way toward the riverbend where the moonlight reflected some shadowy images down among the trees. "They must be okay," he thought. He returned to stoke the campfire, keeping embers alive, but low. Then he too fell asleep.

They were awakened in the morning by the prod of Mayo's boot. "Get moving! Go round up those blamed horses!" he demanded.

"They've scattered!" Hoot said, looking around. "But they'll be just down the trail," he said quickly. "We'll get 'em."

"I told you to bell them! You!" Nick Mayo pointed at Chris. "Go back over the trail, beat the bushes. If you haven't found them all by dark, forget it and catch up to our camp. Leave the runaways to the wolves."

They found the first group about a quarter-mile back, threw bridles on two and went in search of the rest. Fifty-five horses were soon rounded up, including Flash and Hoot's horse, Beetle, but two remained missing and were nowhere to be found. They mounted their own horses and continued the hunt.

"Real fun, searching for two brown horses in a tangle of second-growth poplars and fresh sign everywhere from 55 other horses," Chris muttered as he turned Flash down the trail.

"Sorry," Hoot said, his face red with embarrassment as he read Chris' thoughts. "Uh, I'll see you back at camp. I'll wait up for you." He turned Beetle back on the trail, hollering and swinging his rope to keep the herd on the run and in a straight line back to camp.

"Don't bother. I might not get back 'til midnight," Chris called back.

He wasn't so angry at Hoot as at himself for not following Mayo's orders. They were supposed to be among the top wranglers in the country!

Toward noon Chris ate some cold bannock and drank from a stream. In mid-afternoon the sky darkened and rain began to fall. Still no sign of the horses. Finally, he admitted failure, turned on the trail and headed back to camp, cold, wet, miserable, and tired.

His wet saddle leather creaked and the pouring rain slapped the leaves of trees along the dark trail. Around midnight he crested a hill, and from out the darkness he saw the flicker of a small fire. He recognized it as an Indian camp.

"Hello, the camp!" he called out, in Beaver.

Two men sitting by the fire stood up and returned his greeting.

"Did you see our outfit ride past?"

"Yeah. One of your strays wandered back to our camp."

"Good! I've been looking for those two renegades all day!"

They showed Chris the horse they'd tied to a tree. Sure enough, it was their little bay mare. Chris thanked them, slipped a rope on the mare, then gave her a slap on the rump. "You're a bad one," he said to her. "Bad horses get eaten. Don't forget it."

A few miles later Chris found the second runaway.

By this time, it was nearing two o'clock in the morning. Chris and the three horses plodded on, tired, wet, and hungry. He arrived at the Cache Creek camp as dawn broke over the eastern hills. He dismounted, hitting the ground as stiffly as a wooden soldier, and hunched down to hobble the horses.

Food. He hadn't eaten much all day, except the bannock that tasted like wet leather. Hoot motioned him over and handed him some cold sausages wrapped in pancakes. Chris nodded his thanks, wolfed them down, and crawled into his sleeping bag.

Two hours later the camp was up, and so was Chris.

They awoke to voices cussing. Twenty-two of the 58 animals had gone missing.

"Hoot and Smoky, go back," Mayo ordered.

The runaways were found eight miles down the trail, hardly slowed by the hobbles. The cowboys rounded up the horses and headed them back.

They were greeted by a furious boss. "Are you fellows cowboys or clowns?" Mayo thundered. "You're being well paid for your wrangling knowledge. This kind of thing better not happen again."

"Yes, sir," Hoot said, with a sharp salute.

Mayo did not smile. He wheeled his mule around and started down the trail.

"Some horsemen we turned out to be," Chris said later to Hoot and Skid. "We're going to be fired."

"Yeah?" Skid said. "And where do you think they'd find ten other monkeys out here in the bush?"

Smoky came riding up to them. "You young pups just mind your ps and qs," he warned. "Mayo has no time for jokers."

As the party crossed the Montney Creek bridge, Skid waved, "Good-bye civilization, hello nowhere." For the next hundred miles they'd see no one and it was life or death important that they get along, men and animals.

Chris liked being with the cowboys. Smoky Sloan had a home place on the Wicked River a few miles downstream from Mayo's, but neither of them spent much time there. Both made their living wrangling horses or panning gold in the summer months and running their traplines in the winter.

Smoky smelled of wood smoke and always had a rolled smoke clenched between dark-stained teeth. He was a true mountain man, preferring the outdoors to inside and spreading his bedroll out by the fire rather than inside the tent, the same as Mayo. He didn't join the Commander for his morning swims, however. Each morning the men would watch in amazement as their boss grabbed his sponge, walked down to whatever river, creek, or lake they had camped near, stripped off his clothes and plunged in — even in the pouring rain.

"I've known your folks for a long time," Smoky told Chris one day. "Knew your grandparents, too." He was silent for a moment as if contemplating whether to say anything more. He turned to look at Chris riding beside him. "It's said you're a chosen one."

"What does that mean?"

"Guess you'll know when the time comes." Smoky urged his horse ahead to help a packhorse that had got his pack stuck between two poplars.

Chris considered Smoky's words. He'd always known something unusual had been forecast for his future. His grandmother had told him so, although his parents never talked about it. But he'd seen his mother looking at him with a serious expression, especially when he'd predicted things like the location of game or unexpected weather changes.

"Just dumb luck," Karl Haldane had said and Chris wanted to agree. But it was something more, a gift that Chris's Danish father would never understand. Being of mixed blood Chris often felt pulled in two directions, between the quiet spirituality of his native grandmother and the opposing businesslike attitude of his father.

Chris became more and more curious about Smoky Sloan's and Nick Mayo's friendship, which he felt went back a long way. Both were loners. "I got no one to send Christmas cards to," was how Smoky described his lack of family. Nick Mayo was one of his few friends, but where had they met? "I knew Nick from before," was all Smoky said when asked. "We were business partners. He's odd but he's honest."

Commander Mayo certainly was odd. The boys could barely keep from laughing at his admiration for Rubbish, the perky little black mutt, and Molly his silly old mule. As soon as Molly's pack was removed at the end of the day she would promptly drop to her knees and, grunting happily, roll back and forth in the mud. The next morning Mayo would have to brush her clean before she could be packed, not seeming to mind the extra work or her dismal braying as much as the cowboys' silent smirks.

Mayo seldom smiled, never laughed, and showed few emotions other than disapproval when things went wrong.

Rubbish and Molly seemed to respect that, and they got along famously.

"You had that dog a while?" Chris asked him one day, catching up to him at the head of the party.

"Long enough to teach it a few things," was Mayo's reply.

"Like what?"

Without answering, Mayo reached into a pocket, drew out his wallet and heaved it into the bush. None of the other men saw the action, and the party rode on as usual for a mile or more. Suddenly Mayo stopped, dismounted, and called the dog.

"I've lost my wallet, old chap," he said, as if addressing a friend. "Go find it for me will you? Now that's a good dog."

An hour later the men were finishing their noonday meal of bannock, jam and tea when Rubbish came panting up and dropped the wallet at Mayo's feet. For this piece of work Rubbish received a pat on the head and a piece of bannock. "Well, we can be off," Mayo announced. He looked at Chris and just a hint of a proud smile crossed his face.

They crossed Grayling and Iron creeks, and headed north again up the Halfway River, planning to ford above the forks. They were nearing Mayo's and Smoky's home territory, and luckily both men were familiar with this high, fast water.

"Don't go straight across — water's too deep, the horses would have to swim," Mayo ordered. "Head-and-tail them into groups of four. Raise the packs containing perishables. Follow the riffle upriver before you try to cross."

The men felt pretty good after that crossing. Hoot doffed his hat toward Mayo. "Well done, boss."

The Halfway River switched back and forth across their trail. Some of the horses were inexperienced at fording and drifted with the flow. Hoot and Skid stretched a long rope between their saddle horses, and swung it to keep the ponies moving across in a straight line.

After riding all day, they camped on the lower Beaver Indian reserve at the Halfway River on a wide flat plateau. When night fell and the grass meadow brought hoards of mosquitoes, they made a smoke-fire from green timber. "Great choice. We can sit in the smoke and choke, or sit out of the smoke and be chewed up," Smoky said.

"I don't mind mosquitoes, long as there's no bees," Amoo the cook commented.

"We're getting near the Watson place," Skid said the next morning. "Want to meet the future in-laws?"

Chris reddened. "Get off it," he said, and spurred his horse ahead to the laughter of the men.

"Albert Watson's got a pretty nice place," Smoky said as they trotted along the meadow land. "The Watson land is next to the Turner ranch. Young Turner has always had his eyes on it. Yep, it would sure make a nice chunk of property if you tied those places together. Billy Turner would be the King of the Halfway!"

Smoky managed to look surprised when Chris spurred Flash into a gallop and raced off across the meadow. But Smoky's roar of laughter indicated the old cowboy knew more than he let on about life and love.

SIX
THE LEGEND OF DEAD MAN LAKE

July 14th started with bright sunshine and everyone in a good mood, including the horses. They crossed the swift but shallow Cypress River that flowed from the western mountains, to arrive around suppertime at the Brady homestead on the north side of the river.

Bill Brady had come here from Missouri in 1916. He'd trapped along the Halfway River, then taken up land on the Cypress and opened a little post to trade with the Indians. He'd married a Beaver Indian woman and they were raising their large family in this beautiful place.

The Bradys welcomed the party for supper, so they pastured their horses on a grassy river flat, washed up, and walked to the house. Mrs. Bessie Brady looked at Chris a bit oddly when they were introduced, as if trying to place him in her mind. Later, she approached him. "Your grandparents are Adolphus and Agathe Deschenes?"

"Yes."

She smiled. "You look like your grandfather. He was a Keeper."

"A Keeper?"

"A Keeper of the Cross."

"Oh."

Chris had been told his grandfather was gifted with special powers, but had never met the man as he'd died the year Chris was born. His grandmother always said that Chris would someday follow in his footsteps. Was this what Smoky was referring to? Now, at the thought of his grandfather, Chris felt a compelling urge to return to The Two Mountains That Sit Together. Thoughts churned around in his head.

Supper was a feast of roast beef, potatoes, garden peas, fresh bread, and apple pie. Chris tried to be polite, but after camp meals of stew, spuds and bannock, he couldn't resist filling his plate a third time. There was lots to go around.

After supper one the Brady kids came over to his dad, put his hand into his pocket and pulled out a plug of chewing tobacco. He took a chew, then passed it around so each child, boys and girls from three or four years old up, had a chew. Mrs. Brady chewed also.

"That woman could hit a one-gallon pail from twenty feet, and never spill a drop," Smoky said admiringly. "I saw her do it. Great cook, too."

Later, when they went back to check the horses, Bill Brady came with them. Chris was bending down to check the feet of his saddlehorse when he heard a conversation between Bill Brady and Smoky Sloan. He heard the name "Turner" and was caught between standing up and letting his presence be known, or staying low and quiet. He decided to shut up and listen.

" . . . got nothin' against white people setting up ranches," Brady was saying. "Whites and Indians can get on just fine if they respect each other. Like me and the missus!" he laughed. "But the Turners never learned that."

"Stubborn folk," Smoky acknowledged. "Can't tell them much, Lyle or the kid."

"Well, they're headed for trouble. The wife's relatives been telling us they won't let Indians cross their land!"

A horse whinnied and kicked at another, and Smoky and Bill went over to check them out. Chris made his escape. He didn't want to be caught eavesdropping but couldn't help the feeling of satisfaction he got from knowing he wasn't the only one having troubles with Billy. He hadn't realized that his skin colour might add fuel to the fire of Billy's antagonism. He, too, was glad to be on this trip. "Keep your friends close, and your enemies closer," was his father's advice.

They bought more supplies from the Bradys. Even though their stock was low they supplied the party with flour, beans, salt, rice, coffee, tea and plug tobacco.

The trail next took them through a mountain pass, with Pink Mountain to the north. They dropped gas and food caches at strategic spots that had been plotted out by Bedaux's organizers. It was a relief to get rid of the awkward, heavy gas cans.

They rode on through lush meadows backed to the west by mountains. "This is beautiful country," Chris said. "I wouldn't mind setting up here myself."

"Yeah, but you'd have to become a hermit. Women don't like being 140 miles from the nearest town," Hoot laughed.

"Yeah, like Jessie Watson, for instance," Smoky added with a smile. "Her folks may ranch on the lower Halfway, but she strikes me as a city girl."

"She does?" Chris said. Then he added quickly, "I'm not thinking of Jessie Watson! I'm not thinking of anyone living here but me!" He could feel his face burning. After that, he couldn't stop thinking about Jessie.

Compared to the Turners, what did the Haldanes have? A scrubby trading post on government land, a few log buildings, a newly-registered trapline that was being disputed by various native bands who said it was their land. Even the trading post was being threatened. If it was profitable the Hudson's Bay Company would show up and make them an offer; if the Haldanes refused to sell the Hudson's Bay could set up on the other side of Finlay Bay in competition.

Chris's mood was dark when they neared the Sikanni Chief River and encountered muskeg. First one, then another of the packhorses got stuck up to their bellies with their legs totally submerged. One by one the men had to work through the rain-threatening day to haul them out. Of all the animals only Molly the mule showed any sense. While the horses fought the muskeg, which sucked them down more deeply, Molly "snapped" her feet up and back and pranced through, small hooves and all.

"She's stronger than a horse, pound for pound, and twice as smart," Mayo said proudly.

But once the mule was safely on the far bank she refused to move further until her partner horse, Big George, had flailed his way to shore. She watched him plunging about, and shook her head in disgust, but stayed faithful until he heaved himself up on the bank.

After crossing the rock-strewn Sikanni Chief River, the trail angled past Trimble Creek to Dead Man Lake. They set up camp on the west side of the lake, and Mayo ordered two men to swim out and set a fish net. "We need some variety to our diet," he said, looking at Amoo, who smiled in agreement.

"Maybe you fellows should hear how this lake got its name before someone 'volunteers' to jump in," Smoky drawled.

Mayo scowled, but on urging from the others he began to relate the tale of Dead Man Lake.

"Jack Thomas from Hudson's Hope took on the job guiding two men to their prospecting claim by this lake," Smoky said. "One was a Texan and the other a Mexican. They'd come into the Peace country by the old Edson Trail and got lost. By the time they arrived at the Hope, they were fighting like cats and dogs, blaming each other for messing up.

"Both men were packing revolvers," Smoky went on. "One kept his gun in his hand, never laid it down. The other had his gun slung into a hip holster. Thomas didn't like the situation at all, and at Red River he tried to get them to turn back. 'Nope. We're going on!' They'd stare like hoot owls at Thomas, then at each other, and Thomas saw their hands were never far from their holsters."

The lapping lake, the darkening sky and the ridge of mountains provided an eerie, lonesome background to Smoky's story. Chris glanced around. Nothing but the black night and the occasional jingle of horse bells.

"Every day got worse. They came near to drawing on each other a couple of times, but then one or the other'd drop his hand. Thomas was getting mighty spooked."

He wasn't the only one, thought Chris. He looked around the campfire. The men appeared uneasy, even the usually calm Amoo.

"When they arrived at this here lake, then called Trimble, Thomas refused to take them any farther. He packed enough grub to get himself back to the Hope, and without turning his back on them he left those two pole-cats to fight it out."

Smoky stopped to roll a smoke. The men made no sound. "A day or two later," he continued in a low voice as the men strained to hear, "a mining party came out from Bluebell Mountain and found two bodies on the shore here. The Mexican had a bullet hole between his eyes. The Texan was shot through the heart. The miners formed a 'bush jury' to examine the evidence, conclude what happened, and buried them — right there."

Chris and the others looked to where Smoky pointed. About 50 feet down the lakeshore from their camp were twin piles of stones. The mounds were silhouetted in the silver light of the rising moon. Chris crossed himself and looked away.

"So it's been called Dead Man Lake ever since," Smoky concluded. "Now, which of you fellows is volunteerin' to swim out and fix those fish nets for the boss?"

The men laughed nervously. "Not me," Chris said. "I got lots of respect for legends."

"Not me," said Hoot. "Not me," said Skid. Amoo shook his head

"You bunch of dunderheads!" Mayo thundered. "I thought we'd hired men, not pantywaists!" He stripped off his boots and splashed into the water.

⊷⊱⊶

The dawn came grey, bringing a low mist that hovered above the lake. The men rose from their bedrolls, tired, cold, and hungry. Why was there no fire going? Why wasn't there a pot of coffee set out? Where was Amoo?

Mayo pushed aside Amoo's tent flap and crawled inside. In seconds he backed out, his normally-military voice shaking. "First Aid kit. Right away! What do we have for insect bites? Amoo's unconscious!"

Mayo grabbed the kit and crawled into the tent while the men waited outside. They recalled how Amoo got his nickname, and could only hope it wasn't a bee sting. Chris remembered his grandmother telling him that bee stings caused more deaths than snake bites . . . and Amoo had told them of his allergy.

Chris went over to the tent and knelt down. The thing lying on the low-slung canvas cot didn't resemble Amoo, or even a man. His face was red and puffed, as round as a basketball, and his breath was anguished and wheezing. Mayo was administering some ointment from a bottle, trying to wedge a spoon between Amoo's swollen lips so he wouldn't swallow his tongue and choke to death.

Chris crawled inside. "He knew he was allergic," he said. "He must have some special medicine in his pack."

"Then find it!" Mayo barked. His normally cool appearance had disappeared; his bandanna was soaked with sweat and droplets ran from his chin onto his shirt front.

Chris grabbed Amoo's pack and dug through it, throwing aside clothes, footwear, shaving gear, tooth powder, hair brush. "Here!" he said, holding up a bottle. "It says 'For Insect Stings'. It's some kind of drug— ."

Mayo grabbed the bottle, barely taking time to read the label. Holding it to Amoo's mouth he tipped it up, and in moments the stricken man's breathing eased. "Musta been . . . hiding in my bedroll," he whispered. The words were muffled almost beyond understanding by his swollen tongue and lips, and his eyes were completely shut. He gestured with sausage-fingers toward his neck. There they could see a small black speck — the bee's stinger still marked the area of attack. Taking a penknife, Mayo scraped out the stinger, then snapped an order to Smoky to get some baking soda for a compress.

They held over two days at Dead Man Lake, waiting for Amoo to recover. The emergency had struck them all. Most people who spend time in the wilderness knew that for insect bites you could wipe on a paste of charcoal from the fire, or even urinate on the wound to apply ammonia, but no one had ever dealt with an allergic reaction. It was sobering and scary, even more so on the haunted shore of Dead Man Lake.

SEVEN
THE PROPHET AND THE MUSKWA

The hard day's haul up the mountainside wasn't worth the wear and tear on the horses as far as Chris was concerned, until he saw the view on the other side. A long misty meadow of chest-high grass lay at the foot of a canyon that formed the Prophet River valley. Horse heaven!

"Ain't that a pull on your eyeballs!" said Smoky.

"A natural corral," said Mayo. "Let's go."

To the west was an endless series of glistening white peaks. "I wonder what our chances are of making it through those rocks to the coast?" Chris said to Smoky.

"A lot better with horses than with the cars!" Smoky snorted.

Although they were careful while herding the horses down the steep slope, the trail was treacherous. The hooves of the first horses scraped the moss from the rocks, making the trail almost unnavigable for those that followed. The last horses started to skid, fell back, and slid the rest of the way on their rumps. Two packhorses tripped over roots and went rolling and crashing down the mountainside. Their screams faded to grunts, followed by the clatter of rocks, then silence.

Chris, Skid and Hoot scrambled down to find that large trees had saved the horses from plunging all the way to the bottom. With eyes rolling in fear, they lay, sides heaving and feet helplessly pawing the air. Talking softly to calm them, the cowboys undid the ropes and cinches, and one at a time helped them upright. Amazingly no bones had been broken and no injuries could be seen beyond cuts and bruises. The packs were beat up but not ruined. After being repacked the ponies scrambled back onto the path. After checking and tightening the lash ropes on all the horses, the party continued down the mountainside.

By nightfall, it was raining hard and water began spilling over the riverbanks. The camp was moved to higher ground. In the morning, two inches of water floated in the tents and the new day dawned foggy and wet. After a breakfast of porridge and tea, made by Hoot as Amoo was still weak, Chris and Skid climbed to a rock ledge to scan the valley floor for the horses. They saw none.

"Make a raft," Mayo commanded. "Smoky and I will paddle up the dead floodwater to see if the horses have swum toward the mountains to gain higher ground." He turned to Chris. "Pack your rifle. Find us some meat while you're scouting for high pasture land."

Sure. In the pouring rain.

Chris saddled Flash and started off. Nothing but moss-covered rocks, with scrawny timber jammed into crevices. A small creek they'd crossed earlier had become a mad river. As Chris watched, mud-grey water swept away young trees, old stumps and chunks of earth. No point in crossing to look for pasture on the far side; the horses could never make it.

Further up the mountain he noted sign. When he reached the timberline he might find a caribou. As he climbed, the rain became sleet, then snow. At the summit the ground was white, windswept, and colder than Christmas, but he had a job to do.

It was midnight before he finally straggled into camp. Again, Hoot had stayed up to greet him with hot tea and biscuits.

"Did you sight anything?" Hoot asked.

Chris grinned tiredly and held up his prize — a sack containing ten trout. Then he pointed toward Flash. A goat was draped across his back.

"Looks like we'll have meat and fish with our beans," Hoot laughed.

Amoo grilled the trout for supper and prepared the goat meat. He and Chris both received compliments for the fine food, although the goat was old and tough and took a lot of concentrated chewing.

They had to cross the river four times in order to move camp. Pack saddles were put on the horses without blankets while they swam through the dark, swirling, waters.

"You — get on that big horse over there, what-do-you call him!" Mayo shouted to Skid.

"Dog Meat! You want me to ride Dog Meat!"

"You heard me. That horse has been giving us trouble — won't cross water, bucks and wheels when anyone tries to mount him. If he doesn't learn to behave, he's in the stew!"

Skid threw the saddle onto the big horse and started across. As soon as he hit water, Dog Meat rolled over and went under. Skid gave a yell and threw himself out of the saddle, sputtering and flailing in ice-cold water as twenty horses scrambled their way past him.

Smoky rode up on No-Name and grabbed at Skid's jacket. "Hang on!" he yelled, and pulled him aboard. Skid lunged out of the churning water and clung onto No-Name's saddle. He managed to bring a leg over the horse's haunches and rode to safety as No-Name plunged toward to the far bank. Skid lay down, gasping, on the muddy shore. "I don't know what happened!" he panted. "Dog Meat just went under."

"Nearly took you with him," Smoky said, dismounting. He knelt down. "You all right? You took on a lot of water."

Mayo rode up on Molly. "You hurt?"

Skid shook his head. He was cold, wet, and still out of breath. "This is a tough way to make a living," he panted. "The horse . . . "

"That blasted brute, I knew he'd be trouble right from the start!" Mayo said, "But I didn't think he'd be too darned ornery to even swim!"

"What happened to him . . . " Skid began.

"Heart attack, likely," Smoky said.

"Hoot, retrieve the saddle," was Mayo's next order, all business again.

Hoot and Chris rode downriver looking for the horse, dead or alive, but Dog Meat was never to be seen again.

"Guess he's Wolf-Meat now," said Skid.

"And porcupines and rats will eat the saddle," added Smoky. "Nature's clean-up."

Some of the horses were great trail animals but others were hard to catch so they continued to hobble a few, including a mare they called Meany. When they tried to catch her to remove the hobbles before her swim she jumped into the river. "She's too mean to drown," Hoot said. "Bets on that she'll make it across, hobbles and everything."

He won. The mare lunged out of the water up onto the far bank and shook herself. Then she hobbled up the embankment and was happily grazing when the rest of the men and horses got across.

The party climbed 2,000 feet over moss-covered rock, encountering another sleet storm near the top. They rode single-file along the ridge through clouds so thick and white that Chris couldn't see Flash's ears. An outfit of their size, balanced along the crest of a snow and cloud-covered mountain, could quickly encounter danger. To one side was a sheer drop of 1,000 feet; to the other a huge basin cut into the top of the mountain resulting in another drop-off.

Mayo's military cries, passed man to man through the packtrain, was the link that kept the group in a unit. Even as the fog lifted, there were times when the entire pack-string disappeared in tail-ends of clouds that clung to the mountainside.

"Stop! We've got a hurt horse!" Skid called out as they emerged from the fog. Little Babe, the packhorse, had cut her ankle on some sharp rock and was bleeding badly. When they reached flat ground Chris approached the injured mare, his former riding horse, and talked to her in quiet tones. She seemed to remember the good times they'd had last fall, and stayed quiet. He tied the injured mare, and he and Skid threw her down to layer hot grease into her cut. That stopped the bleeding so they could bandage her leg. She lay quietly, her brown eyes fixed on Chris's face, while they doctored her wound.

"She's a spunky little thing!" Chris noted admiringly. When the operation was over, the mare got up, snorted, limped for a step or two, then walked away without a backward glance at the two surgeons.

"You'd think she'd been to the beauty parlour," Skid commented.

"Yeah. She's not a bad little horse. I rode her last fall. Except for the odd surprise rodeo, she handled pretty well. It's a waste to use her as a packhorse."

"I see some of these saddle horses are showing stress," Skid said. "If one goes lame, we'll remember this little gal."

Mayo rode up. "Once we've dropped the last of the supplies, we'll circle back to meet the Bedaux party," he informed the group. "We'll be riding with them the rest of the way west over the mountains."

"I can't imagine Dudes coming through this kind of country in Citröen cars," Chris said.

"You're being paid to ride, not advise!" Mayo said sharply. "When you meet Bedaux, keep your thoughts to yourself."

They were now in the Muskwa River country, noted for small brush and not much grass. They trailed along the river until arriving at a milky-white stream that rushed down from the mountains. On the far side the grass looked pretty good, so they built a makeshift log bridge to get across. Most of the horses had no trouble crossing, as long as the cracks between the logs could be chinked with mud so they couldn't see the water below.

The Muskwa valley here is narrow, bordered by high mountains, with one trail in and one out.

"Hey!" Mayo called, "We've got company!"

The men halted the packtrain and waited, while toward them rode three men. As they neared, they were recognized as members of the Trail-Cutters party. Chris saw Billy Turner among them.

"The rest of the Trail-Cutters are camped back at Big Bar," the leader, Tommy Wilde, said. "It's a six-mile stretch of river-bottom, a son-of-a-gun to get through. The water's low and it breaks into channels that go every which way, with loose gravel bars in between."

"Yeah, the water zig-zags from side to side down the bar," Billy added authoritatively. "Lots of quicksand." He looked over at Chris, his grey eyes mere slits under his hat-brim. "And you have to cross those channels many times. Lots of chances for a pile-up."

"Well, you blokes got through so you can guide," Mayo said. "Let's go."

Tommy Wilde and his Trail-Cutters party had experienced an even rougher time than the Advance Party as they'd left earlier, the first of April, when there was no new grass for the horses to eat. "All they got was year-old grass, what there was of it," Tommy said. "Caused lots of problems with them wandering at night."

They'd also had some food problems of their own. When they had to ration their remaining flour, sandwiches consisted of two slices of meat holding one slice of bread.

By the first of May, new grass had grown and the group was moving slower due to trail-cutting work so the condition of the horses improved. That's when the men began to suffer. Their orders were to cut trails six feet wide with long curves and as few side-hills as possible. Not easy in mountain country. The men looked tired, but fit. Billy

Turner had developed even stronger sets of muscles, and rode shirtless to show off the minute the sun came out.

After a few miles Mayo went back to check some of the packhorses, leaving Chris and Billy in the lead, with Billy riding along the bank. "This river changes every day," he said, displaying his water-reading ability. "Real tricky."

Suddenly the bank gave way and Billy disappeared into the river — saddlehorse, packhorse and all.

Chris could do nothing but helplessly watch. Billy's horse was into deep water immediately and spinning downstream, but the packhorse had retained its footing. For some foolish reason, Billy had hooked the packhorse lead around his wrist. He was about to be yanked from his saddle when the packhorse, too, foundered in deep water. All three were swept away, with Billy struggling between two panicked horses in the swift, churning water.

Chris spurred Flash into a gallop and raced toward a sharp bend in the river. Billy and the horses were riding with the current, which brought them closer to shore. As they came swirling downstream, Chris looped his rope around Billy's shoulders and pulled him from the thrashing horse. He dallied the rope around his saddle horn and urged Flash back, dragging a mud-covered, swearing and hollering cowboy up onto the bank.

The others had now caught up to them. Seeing that Chris had the situation in hand, they sat back on their horses to watch the show. The men cheered as Billy stumbled to his feet, swearing mightily.

"Pretty good pipes for a drowned rat," commented Smoky.

"I guess young Billy has some more to learn about reading rivers," Mayo said. The men laughed, which didn't improve Billy's mood. He didn't even thank Chris for the rope work.

The next morning they reached Emerald Lake where they were met by Bert Bradley, second in command of the expedition.

"The Bedaux party has given up the idea of getting through with half-track vehicles," he announced. "They're abandoning them and plan to make the rest of the trip with horses. All you fellas are to come back and join the main outfit, right now."

"We're finally going to meet the famous Monsieur Bedaux!" Chris said excitedly to Smoky. He spurred his horse to ride near Bradley and Mayo, and hear the latest news.

"It wasn't too bad for the first twenty miles from Fort St. John, but from there we had to travel on a rough, narrow, pack trail," Bradley reported. "Those vehicles were useless crossing creeks, or gullies, or muskeg! One day it took four hours to go a quarter-mile! We had to lever the Citröens with block and tackle through a 300-yard swamp."

He spat into the dust in disgust, recalling the effort. "And they're real gas-gobblers, too," he added. "We finally wised up and abandoned cars numbered One and Two about 50 miles out, at the lower Indian reserve on the Halfway River.

The expedition had gone another 25 miles, with three vehicles winching and bumping their way along, until they reached the forks on the Halfway. That was when Bedaux was informed that they'd come over the easiest part of the trail.

Chris's first sighting of the Bedaux party was of a cameraman with his lens aimed toward him. The cowboys pulled back, aware of their scruffy, beat-up appearance. Coming toward them on horseback was a well-dressed, keen-eyed man of about 50 years, whose manner expressed power and control.

No one needed to be told they were finally meeting Monsieur Charles Bedaux.

EIGHT
DUDES

"*Bienvenue*," said Monsieur Bedaux. "Welcome! I am pleased that we can all finally meet. Most of the Trail-Cutters' crew are already here. Just throw your string of horses in with theirs."

The Advance Party's packstring snorted and pranced as they encountered the other horses. The combined herd of 58 from the Advance Party, 33 from the Trail-Cutters, and 47 from Bedaux's group, totaled 138 horses in all.

As the cooks set up a banquet, the cowboys looked over the camp. "This expedition has more stock than the biggest store in Fort St. John!" Chris marvelled.

The cowboys milled about viewing piles of folding aluminum camp tables, chairs, beds, basins, bowls, bush toilets and bathtubs. There were rugs, cushions, blankets, pillows and mosquito nets. The Dudes' private cook tent was equipped with fancy French cooking pots, crystal glasses, silver cutlery and serving trays.

"How do you like our new load?" Smoky asked Chris, pointing to the women's luggage. "Imagine packing that over hundreds of miles of trails." He shook his head in disgust as he peered at the mound of packs labeled Shoes, Lingerie, Sweaters, Parkas, Pants, Jackets. Bulkier packs contained stoves, folding tables, chairs, beds and bathtubs, heavy cast-iron pots and pans, China dishes and crystal glasses, and cases of top-grade rum and champagne. Other packs carried 200 pounds of French novels.

The cowboys looked on in dismay as they imagined them and the horses struggling through thick forest and over rocky crags transporting this foolish cargo.

"It still might be easier carrying this stuff than those gas cans," Chris said.

"And it smells nicer, too!" Skid added. "Whew! French perfume! The horses will go crazy."

"Long as you don't follow them," Smoky said. "Remember, keep away from the Dudes. No cozying up to any of them. We're workers, not royalty."

Chris looked around at the food supplies. Besides regular fare were cases labeled Mum's French champagne, pâté de foie gras, caviar, smoked salmon, truffles, and chicken-liver pâté. Eight thousand pounds of supplies — all to be packed on horses through mountain trails and across numerous rivers. And unpacked every night.

As the cooks prepared the feast, Bedaux brought out several bottles of rum and passed around cigarettes, pipes, chewing tobacco, soft drinks and chewing gum.

He then called everyone together and asked his party to form a receiving line. He gallantly introduced his wife, "the charming Madame Fern Bedaux"; then her maid Josephine Daly, a roly-poly lady with a nice friendly smile; and a beautiful companion, Bilonha Chiesa.

But the person who caught Chris' eye was a girl a bit older than himself, likely around eighteen. "This is Katrin Bouvier, my wife's cousin," said Monsieur Bedaux with pride in his voice.

Katrin smiled at the assembled group. "You can call me Kati," she said. "That's less formal."

Everyone lined up to shake hands with the Dudes. As Chris took Kati's hand he looked into smiling hazel eyes, then down at their clasped hands. Hers were soft and white, his rough and scarred. He flushed and removed his hand, putting it behind his back. She smiled, "Pleased to meet you," and turned to the next cowboy in line, who was Hoot.

"Kati made sweet eyes at you," Hoot said as they passed down the line. "She didn't even see me! I could have been Santa Claus and she wouldn't have noticed."

Chris felt his face turn crimson.

Billy Turner hadn't been so shy. When it was his turn to meet Kati, he'd lifted up her hand and kissed it.

"That boy came prepared," laughed Smoky. "I saw him using a little tin mirror to shave, and slick back his hair with Vaseline."

Chris laughed. "I would have used bear grease if I'd thought of it. She'd never forget me!"

They were also introduced to Jack Bocock, a geologist and mining engineer, and John Chisholm, a big Scotsman who was Bedaux's personal valet as well as policeman for the expedition. "Big John" had formerly worked as Bedaux's gamekeeper at his villa in France.

"I'll bet one of his jobs is to keep us away from the ladies!" Tommy Wilde noted. Like Billy, he had taken the time to shine up. He wore a bright blue shirt with silver collar tabs, a belt fronted by shining silver buckle, and a clean, tan-coloured, felt hat with a feather band. The cowboys knew and liked Tommy, a showman with a lot of talent both for serious wrangling and making difficult stunts appear easy.

They met geographer Frank Swannell and his assistant, who had been hired to make maps of the expedition, as well as Charles Balourdet, a French mechanic on loan from the Citröen car company.

"Could you show us the cars?" Mayo asked. "I think the lads are pretty curious about them."

"*Certainement!*" Monsieur Balourdet took the group over to the vehicles, in reality tractor units. Caterpillar track drives were mounted on the back with balloon tires on the front. A drum had been installed between the front wheels supposedly to propel them through muskeg and over stumps, rocks and windfall trees.

"They are equipped with ten-horsepower motors with a top speed of twenty miles per hour — an amazing rate for wilderness trails, but quite slow on good roads," Balourdet explained in French-accented English.

"We started off with five vehicles, but as you can see only three have made it this far. Your Canadian wilderness is too rugged for these vehicles."

Chris recalled Einar Olson's comment about the difference between crossing deserts and mountains. Funny how the old prospector could see clearly what Bedaux and Balourdet had yet to learn.

As the men looked over the vehicles, Chris saw Kati standing over by one of the tables. Taking a deep breath, he walked up to her, curiosity overcoming shyness.

"What are those guys doing with cameras?" he asked. "I see them everywhere!"

"Oh, they're movie people from Hollywood," she explained. "Uncle Charles contacted a producer in Los

Angeles and hired their very best filmmakers. They are making a movie of this expedition, so Uncle can sell it and recoup some of his expenses."

"Would people pay to see a movie like this?" Chris asked.

Kati looked at him and smiled. Chris became suddenly aware that he, too, should have used that tin mirror.

"Oh yes!" she replied. "Mr. Crosby won an Academy Award for cinematography on Tabu, you know."

"I saw it in Vancouver. It's set in the South Sea Islands, isn't it?"

Kati looked at Chris with interest. "Vancouver? You're not from around here, then?"

"I was born here. But we get out once in a while!" He grinned at her. It was then he noticed the watchful scowl of Big John. He tipped his hat, "See you later," and moved away.

Everywhere the cowboys went they were followed by Crosby and his assistant, Evan Withrow, and their whirring cameras. The cowboys became nervous — all but Billy Turner and Tommy Wilde who were happy to pose for the camera. Billy seemed unaware that Big John's eyes never left him.

After a fine supper, and drinks of rum for those who wanted it — Billy lined up several times to refill his tin cup — Bedaux told the men a bit about himself and how he'd come here.

"My work has involved reorganizing industrial plants all over the world," Bedaux said. "I developed a system known as 'Equivalism', which means 'production versus consumption, measured in units of equal value.'" Noting the blank looks, he laughed. "It's all about free enterprise.

You do work for me so I can accomplish my goals. For that, I pay you an equivalent value in money, for your expertise and labour."

"I think he's getting the short end of the deal," Smoky said as he downed his third tot of rum. "No outfit I've ever worked for paid this good."

"Same here," Chris agreed.

"This is the third expedition I've made," Bedaux added. "The first was through the Steppes of Russia. The second was across the Sahara Desert of North Africa, driving 10,000 miles from Mombassa on the Indian Ocean, to Casablanca on the Atlantic. We used a combination of wheel and track, similar to the vehicles we brought here."

"What made you decide to try them in the bush country of British Columbia?" Smoky asked.

"I made one trip here two years ago, and found it to be one of the most beautiful, primitive, and challenging areas of the world," Bedaux responded. "So, I organized this expedition through your Canadian and BC governments. André Citröen, who owns the Citröen Tractor Company in France, donated five half-track Citröens, and I had them shipped to Edmonton. As you can see, they're a bit fancier than army 'jeeps'."

He unrolled an oilskin map showing the planned route: 130 miles up the Halfway to the headwaters of the Muskwa River. Then to the main range of the Rocky Mountains, down the White Water (Kwadecha) River to the Finlay, and up to the Fox or Sifton passes. They'd follow the ridge northwest to Dease Lake, west to Telegraph Creek on the Stikine River, down the Stikine to the coast, and back by way of Vancouver.

"We heard your original plan wasn't working," Mayo said, "and you're exchanging autos for horses."

"I'm afraid you're right," Bedaux conceded. "It's the clay 'gumbo'. The treads slipped off, everything got clogged, transmissions, differentials, brake drums. . ."

"Why would you even try to make the trip with cars when you'd bought all these good horses?" Chris asked.

Bedaux looked him in the eye. "Because it has never been done before!" he said emphatically. "Now, I wish you all a good night."

As Chris rode on night herd, he looked back at the camp. It resembled a movie set, not real, like it could be struck in moments. He hoped that Bedaux hadn't taken his comment as criticism, and decided he should have listened better to Mayo's advice. As the Commander had said, they were being paid for wrangling, not mouthing off.

As sleep drifted in Chris thought of Kati, so out of place in this rough country. She was obviously a city-bred girl. Someone said that Madame had brought her along as a favour to Kati's mother. Was she seeking adventure, too? Or was she running away from something back home? He wondered if she had a boyfriend in the States.

NINE
MAKING MOVIES

For Bedaux, nothing was lost. If he couldn't take the Citröens on the trip, they'd be props in an action movie.

"We're pushing two cars over the cliff to plunge headlong into the river," Bedaux directed. "Some crew members — a couple of you cowboys — will jump for your lives as the vehicles clear the bank!"

A perfect setting had been selected for this drama — a 120-foot high bluff overlooking the Halfway River.

"You — and you!" Bedaux said, pointing to Chris and Billy. "Into the cars. Drive toward the cliff. As you approach, throw them into neutral and jump clear."

Chris felt a shot of adrenaline. "Race you to the river!" he yelled to Billy, and sprinted for the cars.

Evan Withrow had set up a camera on the brow of the hill and Swannell had one down below near the river's edge. Crosby operated a third from the far side of the river.

"Okay, this is it," Chris thought. He looked west toward the hazy peaks of the Rockies, then focused on the hood of the Citröen. The engines roared to life. Bedaux stood to the right, a red scarf held high. With a slashing motion, he whipped it around and down. Engines screamed and the cars took off like rocket ships. Chris saw nothing but blue sky. He was airborne.

Then the thought hit him. "I gotta get out!" With a tremendous push he threw himself from the vehicle. He hit the ground rolling and the engines became a distant whine. Chris lay on the ground, gasping as air slowly returned to his lungs. Voices approached. Strong arms pulled him to a sitting position. He looked into the worried face of Hoot.

"Where's Billy?" was Chris's first question.

"He's all right. What about you?" Hoot knelt beside him and swiped some dirt from Chris's hair. Skid picked up Chris's cowboy hat and dusted it off.

"Billy jumped too early," Skid said. "Ruined the shot."

"You want a job in the movies, son?" Chris looked up to see Bedaux standing over him.

Bedaux knelt down. "You were very good," he said. "A natural." He handed him his hat, retrieved from Skid. "I own a film company in France. We'll talk."

"Rum all 'round," he cried. The crowd cheered.

Later, Chris saw Billy approach Charles Bedaux, who turned to glance back at him, frowning.

Smoky was also watching the scene. "I'd like to be a fly on the wall and catch that conversation," he muttered.

"Maybe he's going to fire him," Chris said.

"Nah, he's too good of a cowboy, even with his sour-puss attitude."

Ten minutes later, Billy and Bedaux emerged from the tent and Bedaux barked an order to the crew. "We're moving camp — *immédiatement!*"

Chris and Smoky went over to the corral with the others to begin the long task of saddling, packing, and moving the mountains of equipment. As Chris walked past where Billy stood, Billy put out a hand to stop him. Chris whirled around.

"There's more than one way to skin a cat, and a cowboy," Billy said evenly. "I'd watch my step around here if I was you. You're not the hero you'd like to think you are."

In a reaction Chris shoved, and the unsuspecting cowboy reeled back, catching his balance on the rungs of the pole corral. "Why you!" Billy came back headfirst into Chris' chest. Both cowboys hit the dirt, rolling. The horses snorted, reared, and raced around in a frenzy.

"What the . . . " Smoky grabbed Chris by the belt as Hoot and Skid grabbed Billy, yanking them apart and upright. The fighters leaned back against the corral poles, panting, covered with dust.

Bedaux pushed through the crowd that had gathered. "You — and you!" Bedaux sputtered. "To the tent, now! *Vite! Vite!*"

Chris grabbed his hat from the ground, slapped the dirt from it against his knee, and followed as Bedaux marched ahead, fury shaking his shoulders. He could hear Billy shuffling along behind him.

Once inside the tent, Bedaux whirled to face them. "What do you two miscreants think you're doing, fighting on my time, in my corral, disturbing my people and my horses?" He turned a furious eye on Chris. "And I don't like the things I've been hearing about you — trying some voodoo stuff on the horses, making them rear and pitch certain riders —"

"What?"

" — and saying you're special, have some kind of strange powers!"

"What?"

"Everyone here is equal!" Bedaux thundered. "That's the rule! You are on my payroll and you'll behave like gentlemen or you're gone. It's 100 miles back to civilization but if there's any more fighting I'll turn you out with a horse and some food and you can fight with the bears and wolves."

Chris and Billy turned to look at each other, then both dropped their eyes.

"Shake hands or you're both fired," Bedaux said quietly. "You can pack up and do all the fighting you want on the trail home."

Slowly, Chris extended his hand, and Billy did the same, then withdrawing as if each held a snake.

"Good. Now, get to work."

They moved camp to the far side of the river in three loads, using a specially-built raft set on rubber floats. A cable and winch were strung across the river to guide the raft. It took until nearly midnight and the men were ready to drop, except for Bedaux whose light burned inside his big tent for most of the night.

Bedaux had brought a typewriter, a heavy and awkward thing to carry by packhorse, and he regularly sent a rider back to Fort St. John with typewritten stories chronicling events of the expedition. His crazy mix of fact and fantasy was duly sent by wire, to be reported in newspapers and broadcast over radio stations in New York, London, and Paris. He wrote of crew members mysteriously disappearing when actually a cowboy had left the expedition to stay on a ranch they'd passed by. When he heard the story of how Dog-Meat drowned, Bedaux reported that a man had drowned.

Chris managed to write a couple of short letters to Jessie, and send them out with the dispatch rider.

You wanted to know about the women on this trip. For one, they can't ride. Madame Fern is the best, much better than Mesdames Bilonha and Josephine (see, I'm learning French!). Mademoiselle Katie will learn with time — your pal Billy has volunteered to teach her! — but Madame Josephine hangs onto the reins like a tug-of-war, pulling and yanking until her poor horse finally decided to teach her a lesson. We were crossing a stream, not deep, when the mare slowly turned over onto its side. We came to the rescue, but Smoky decided it was time to give her a riding lesson, and she knew it was time to listen.

He stopped writing, and looked around. The scene was fantastic, sun shining, bees buzzing, birds calling, and the usual hum of activity over at the corrals, repairing, repacking. He thought of home, and of his folks running the little post. He thought of Hudson's Hope 90 miles downstream, a picturesque village on a plateau over-looking the Peace River. He pictured Jessie studying, writing exams, then he saw himself in Vancouver doing the same. Would he go back?

A sudden image came to him of the Two Mountains That Sit Together. The twin peaks sat like lighthouses above the network of rivers that joined to form the Peace.

He glanced down at the paper in front of him. Well, he couldn't just send information, he'd have to write something about his feelings. But, what were they?

I think of you often, especially at night when the camp is quiet, with just an old owl hooting in a hollow tree. The nights have been warm even this far into the mountains, and most of us sleep outside rather than in the tents, except when it rains of course. The other night we had a real show of Northern Lights, like the night we watched them, coming home from the dance.

He noticed that the rider was nearly ready to leave with Bedaux's latest dispatch. He hurriedly wrote *Love, Chris* and sealed the envelope.

They were now a big outfit so progress was slow, and soon the morning air began to carry the dreaded hint of frost. No one was surprised when on August 17th Bedaux made an announcement.

"It is getting late in the season. With the Citröens abandoned only a pack trail is needed. Messieurs Ernest Lamarque, a land surveyor, and Jack Stone, a native guide from the coast, will go ahead to mark out an overland trail west to Dease Lake and Telegraph Creek. Some members of the Trail-Cutters party will follow to widen the trail and cut brush."

Bedaux's new plan divided the outfit into sections: each two packers would look after twelve packhorses. Chris was partnered with Nick Mayo.

When the party was ready to mount, Bedaux would loudly call, "*Aux chevals!*"

"That's a military order," Mayo explained. "It means, 'on your horses'."

When he wished the party to dismount, Bedaux called, "*Aux pieds!* On your feet!"

The cowboys laughed among themselves. "Look at the little pipsqueak," Smoky snorted. "Stands five foot six, with a voice like a trumpet."

"Don't forget, Monsieur Bedaux was in the French Foreign Legion! He's a crack shot and a good captain," Mayo said, with a smile.

As Chris packed, he watched the precision with which Mayo did his work. "You were in the military?" he asked, hoping to hear a few good stories.

"I was," Mayo said curtly.

"Were you in action?"

"Yes." Mayo turned to hang panniers on a skittish little horse who'd had enough of carrying foolish things.

"Where?"

"Dardanelles. Zeebrugge."

"Doing what?"

"Commanded a destroyer."

"That must have been exciting."

"Wasn't." Mayo turned to Chris. "We formed an expeditionary force to capture the Gallipoli Peninsula and Constantinople in Turkey. But the blighters had salted the straits with explosive mines. That's why I hate civilization and I have no use for most people on this earth."

The expedition trekked over the Caribou range, more than 100 horses in three sections, strung out a mile above treeline. The sun shone, and the horses were rested and perky. At one point Chris could see three separate waterways, all with their headwaters cascading from the high western mountains.

But even as he admired the beauty, his thoughts turned to the practical side: they were facing a rough trail and autumn was swiftly approaching. Some of the Dudes' party were totally inexperienced riders. Madame Josephine still crossed rivers clenching for dear life onto high-held reins, eyes shut tight as her horse plunged straight up the middle of the current. Mesdames Bilonha and Fern were better horsewomen, but the long days, especially when it was rainy and cold, were hard on them. Kati struggled with her horse, and had changed mounts three times, each time asking for a more quiet horse. Even so, she was beginning to look exhausted.

Chris rode up to her after one particularly difficult crossing. "Can I give you a hand?" he asked. "Maybe I could ride beside you, kind of coach your horse across."

She looked around. "It's not allowed. Billy Turner already asked. I thought Big John was going to knock his head off."

He rode away, but couldn't help but wonder whose orders Big John was following — Bedaux's or his own. But, until something happened, he had a job to do and it wasn't to escort ladies.

Whenever the expedition came to a difficult crossing, the cameramen would race ahead to perch at the "bad spots" on the trail, ready to catch some misadventure. "No cussing!" Mayo warned the men.

They arrived at Goat Gulch where the rocky trail angles steeply into a ravine and just as steeply juts up the far side. "Watch Molly," Mayo said. The mule looked down at the ravine to size up the situation, then carefully placed each tiny hoof, testing the footing before setting down her full weight. In contrast, the horses plunged and puffed. At the end of the climb, they were winded and sweating. Molly was damp and breathing deeply, but not panting.

"Well, I declare, that mule is a wonder!" Smoky said.

"I told you so!" Mayo said, smiling happily.

On the first of September they arrived at Emerald Lake at the head of the Muskwa River. Swannell renamed the pretty lake Fern, in honour of Madame Bedaux. He then proceeded to name the highest snow-covered peak Mount Bedaux, and various mountains in the area after others in the Bedaux party.

"The country's changing, right before our eyes," Smoky commented.

TEN
DECISION DAY

"Sometimes," Chris thought, "I'm more aware of what is happening with nature than with people."

He noticed the frost in the air, and the leaves exchange green for gold. Every day he saw the snowcaps droop farther down the mountains. Animals spotted along the trail were at the peak of their summer prime.

Bedaux was in good humour, and excitedly oversaw a film project he called "Adventures on the Trail".

First, they suspended a barrel lengthwise on ropes between trees to represent a bucking bronc. Tommy Wilde, dressed in his flashiest outfit, rode the "bronc" while the audience yelled encouragement as directed. But the cowboys' cheers soon turned to groans when they were asked to saddle 25 horses for the next scene.

"Hang anything on them for packs," Crosby directed. "In fact, put some on so they're sure to fall off. The action tonight will depict a forest fire roaring in to camp!"

"Is he nuts?" Chris asked.

"Yep," was Smoky's response.

The men were told to plant flares and smoke bombs throughout the camp, which would be lit at a signal from the director. "Now, dash around, pull down the tents, and throw everything onto the horses!" Crosby said. "Shoot your revolvers into the air to spook the horses."

In minutes, it was over. The smoke cleared, flares died out, and the horses had all disappeared.

"Go get them," said Bedaux, sounding more tired than amused.

It was pitch dark and raining by the time all the horses were found. Chris had just rounded up the last horse and hauled the saddle off its rainsoaked back, when Monsieur Bedaux approached him.

"I've been watching you handle these animals," he said. "You show a natural ability, and your appearance is right."

"It is? For what?"

"For film," he said. "The Canadian native image is very popular in Europe. I'd like you to consider doing some movie work for me next year in France. It will pay well, and you'll have fun. I've been around a lot of horsemen, and I've seldom seen anyone handle them like you do."

"I don't speak French very well."

"The horses won't care — I ship them over from Canada!" he laughed. "You'll pick up the language. Some of the people here could teach you. But your roles will mainly involve action scenes."

"Oh."

When Chris finally crawled into his bedroll, he was cold and the bed felt damp. He should have been so tired that he'd drop off immediately, but instead he lay awake staring into the dark, listening to raindrops patter on the tent roof, and thinking about the exciting offer of movie work.

As he tossed and turned in his bed, he made up his mind. When the expedition was over he would go to The Two

Mountains That Sit Together, and stay until he found some answers.

⟞✦⟝

The little black mongrel, Rubbish, had won the hearts of the entire expedition. He had a happy face and dancing black eyes. Although his tail wagged furiously when someone paid him attention, he was completely devoted to Commander Mayo. Rubbish was often praised as a hero when he'd come panting up to the party carrying in his mouth an article that someone had dropped or left behind on the trail — a glove, jacket or saddle blanket. In spite of his popularity no one sneaked him food, not even the women of the Bedaux party who made a fuss of him in every other way. Mayo made it plain that it was strictly forbidden for anyone but him to feed Rubbish.

One day the skies opened up and cold rain, then hail, came pelting down. The hailstones bounced off Mayo's bandanna-covered head but he stoically walked along seeming not to notice, refusing to put on any protective headgear, and leading the reluctant Molly.

They had come into some heavy brush and Mayo, leading the party, expertly slashed with his machete at the buck-brush and Devil's Club blocking the trail. Suddenly there sounded a short sharp yelp of pain. Chris drew in his horse as Mayo suddenly fell to the ground in front of him and gathered something in his arms. It was Rubbish. Mayo's machete had sliced through the dog's neck when he'd run through the brush and come too close to the slashing blade.

Chris jumped off his horse. "My God!" but Mayo signaled him away. Chris ran back and put up a hand to slow the party so the Dudes wouldn't witness the scene. Smoky rode over to Mayo and the two exchanged glances. Smoky dismounted and the two men walked off the trail into the trees. In moments a shot was heard. Smoky emerged and a few minutes later Mayo followed. He was covered in blood and his usually tanned face was ghostly white. Chris and Smoky stayed behind and dug a hole at the side of the trail to bury the faithful little mutt.

"Never seen that man show any emotion 'til today," Smoky said. "He loved that dog."

The trail became just plain miserable, yet the party laboured on, into country suitable only for mountain goats. Another horse was lost on a narrow trail that wound around the edge of a steep ravine. When its pack bumped against a rock, the packhorse lost its footing and plummeted 60 feet, breaking a leg. Smoky was elected to finish him off.

Chris recalled Skid's warning, "This expedition is going to be hard on the horses." Had they known, would any of these horsemen signed up? Likely. It was a Depression, and they were earning money that would feed their families for many months.

On September 10th they were an hour out of camp heading toward White Water River — locally called Kwadacha — when two packhorses lost their footing. Down a mud bank they plummeted, rolling and screaming, to splash into the river. It was impossible to rescue them in the pack-high water. The river current swept them into the mainstream, and the cowboys could only watch as the horses went bobbing around a bend out of sight.

Billy was the first to swing into action. "Let's go!" he yelled.

Skid and Chris urged their horses into a gallop in the hope of intercepting the horses at a tight bend. There would be only minutes to make a rescue. Into the ice-cold water they plunged, chaps and all. As the two packhorses swam past, the men were able to snap ropes onto their halter shanks and pull them back into shallow water. The frightened ponies shivered and shook as Billy, Skid and Chris unpacked them and dragged the waterlogged packs up onto the bank. By that time, both men and horses were dead beat and chilled to the bone. Skid built a fire and they all hovered around to feel its warmth through stiff, cold, clothes.

When they'd dried off and their teeth had stopped chattering, they began to sort out the packs. Billy began tossing soggy piles of paper from one of the packs onto the ground. "Just some writing junk," he said disgustedly. "Even too wet to burn good."

"They're notes and maps!" Chris said. "Let's have a look."

"What for?" Billy said, disinterested.

"We can dry them out," Skid said. "They should be okay if we can get them apart while they're wet. Maybe they're important." He took the papers out one by one and carefully spread them over canvas to dry. The waterlogged packs contained notes and sketches of maps, now smudged and some nearly illegible.

By the time the rest of the group reached them, the notes had been dried and stacked near the fire.

"What happened here?" Bedaux demanded. "The notes, maps — did they get — ?"

"They're okay, Mr. Bedaux," Billy said. "I made sure they got dried out good."

"Oh, fine, fine! Thank you so very much."

Skid and Chris exchanged looks.

⊰✥⊱

It was an interesting mix of people in the three groups. The Trail-Cutters and Advance Party were comprised of men who knew the wilderness — packers, guides and wranglers — while the Dudes and their accomplices were from the cities of the world. Sometimes they showed great admiration for the beauty around them, and sometimes not.

One day when the party had decided to stay over to rest the horses, the French mechanic, Balourdet, asked one of the cowboys to take him fishing. Chris was elected. He took him to a small stream where he knew there were lots of trout, in fact they could see them swimming around in a nice clear pool, but they got no bites. "We will have fish for supper!" Balourdet announced. He went back to the camp and returned with a stick of dynamite, a cap and a fuse. Chris watched, saying nothing, as the mechanic set up the charge. Then they took shelter behind the bank and Balourdet let it go. Bang! Up flew water, gravel and fish. "There, see? That's how you catch fish!"

The anger mounted in Chris. But, Balourdet was one of Bedaux's special friends, and he remembered Mayo's orders: see, hear, don't speak.

That night, the cowboys felt exhausted and low in spirit. It had been a hard trail, and they were getting into some deep mountain country. Worse, they had over half the journey yet to go. It was now the 12th of September, and this high up snow could come any time.

As Chris ate his supper of rice, beef and biscuits, he felt downhearted about a number of things. He pitched his meal scraps into the fire and wandered over to where the horses were tethered. He watched them try to graze on the meagre high-altitude grass. He heard a footstep and turned to see Smoky. "I'm beginning to hate this," Chris said.

"We're one good day's travel from Fort Ware," Smoky replied. "Get a break there."

"Good. I'll be glad to see some human beings aside from this bunch, no offense meant."

"None taken," Smoky drawled, rolling a smoke.

"Maybe this isn't the life for me," Chris said slowly. "When I came home from school last year I was told there wasn't enough money to send me back. This job seemed like a godsend. Now, I don't know."

"Tell you what, Wrangler," Smoky said. "You got lots of time to think about your future. Take a look at those Dudes, then check out the cowhands. Figure what got us where we are, then make your plan."

Chris looked at Smoky with admiration. "I couldn't have got better advice from my own father. Thanks."

"Don't mention it."

Smoky bent to check a pony's foot and swore when he saw the beginning of hoof rot. Chris picked up the foot of another horse and matched Smoky's expletive. Infection had broken out along the hairline of the hoof. If untreated the hoof would eventually fall off. The only medicine they had was a salve called Blue Stone that would have helped some if the horse's feet could be kept dry until they healed. But there was no chance to do this on the trail.

"Kid, why don't you hike back to the supply tent for some of that Blue Stone? You and I can be horse-doctors for a while. Don't let Bedaux know. It ain't his problem. Yet."

In the morning the sky was blind-white and the ground covered with two inches of wet snow. "At least the horses stayed close," Smoky remarked. Following a fast breakfast, they packed up and hit the wet, cold, slippery trail to Fort Ware.

Chris's saddle leather creaked, his hat brim filled with wet snow, and his knees ached from being held in the same position for mile after mile. He thought again of Bedaux's offer of work in the movies. From what he'd heard from the other guys, Bedaux's word was good. His travelling companions must have been having similar thoughts as they rode along ahead. He could see their backs, dark with damp, hunched over in their saddles as the horses plodded through snow-covered trails.

He recalled the packs getting wet from the river-dunking, and how Bedaux had been so anxious to preserve the precious notes and diagrams, and keep them from prying eyes. Maybe the maps were what this trip was all about. But why were they so important? Just who was Monsieur Bedaux?

He felt a horse and rider edge up beside him, and through the mist-shrouded rain he saw Billy Turner. Billy grinned over at Chris.

"That was some nice rescue work yesterday, with the horses in the river," he said.

Chris nodded.

"No hard feelings about the other day, eh Haldane?"

Chris waited, watching the trail ahead, trying to keep his face expressionless.

"I guess this will be the last time we'll ride together," Billy added.

Chris looked over at him.

"I've been offered something more interesting than sharing a lousy tent and a muddy trail with a pack of cowhands," Billy said. He smiled again. "Bedaux has offered me a job in the movies!"

ELEVEN

FORT WARE

When Chris rode in to Fort Ware, he felt at home. Camped around the post were several Sikanni Indian families. He greeted them, and received news that all was fine at The Forks.

One of the boys, Johnny Pierre, came over to the corral. "So, what do you think of our Dudes?" Chris asked, grinning. "Did you get them bedded down okay?"

"Yeah, sure," Johnny laughed. "Jimmy Ware gave his cabin to the main group and everyone else just spread their bedrolls on the floors." He indicated the warehouse and the small store. "They didn't like it much."

"What's the matter with dry plank floors? Better than sleeping out in the bush like we've been doing."

"Not fancy enough, I guess," Johnny said with a shrug. "The ladies complained. I guess they're used to better things, even on the trail."

"You've got that right! Wait till you see what we're packing," Chris said, laughing. "Feather beds, bath tubs . . . "

"No kidding?" Johnny grinned. "Well, I hope you don't mind the warehouse floor. That's where we've been told to throw your stuff."

"Looks good to me," Chris said. The tiredness of the trail was beginning to hit him. "In fact, I'm real ready to catch 40 winks."

"Better not turn in yet," Johnny said. "Your boss has a big surprise for you guys. You're gonna like it!"

After the horses had been unpacked and turned loose to graze, the cowboys were summoned to camp head-quarters, a large tent that contained a kitchen.

"Fort Ware will be our pivotal point," Bedaux announced. "You know that Messieurs Lamarque and Stone left one month ago to blaze a trail through to Telegraph Creek. We will wait here for their return. They will either come in person or send a message to let us know what chance we have, and the best route, if we are to continue our journey. At that time I'll decide whether to go ahead or abandon the venture and send everyone home by boat down the Finlay."

A ton of extra supplies ordered earlier had been freighted up the Finlay River to Fort Ware, and was now stacked to the rafters in the warehouse. Because it was so late in the season, and the horses were exhausted and already overloaded, Bedaux decided to lighten the freight rather than add to it. The best way to use up a mountain of food was to put on a big feast.

When the cowboys saw the cooks set platter after platter on the long tables they couldn't believe it was all for them.

"*Pour l'apéritif*," Monsieur Bedaux announced, "we shall have caviar!" He then demonstrated how to spoon some of the dark red mass onto a little bitty piece of toast. Everyone laughed as Bedaux licked his lips and rubbed his stomach in delight.

"You try it first," Hoot said, pushing Chris ahead. "I don't like food that jiggles."

The jellied mounds resembled fish eggs that Chris had seen clustered at the edge of a lake. "What is caviar?" he quietly asked Amoo.

"Sturgeon eggs!" Amoo said. "Brain food!"

With all eyes on him, including Kati's, Chris carefully spooned some onto the toast. He gulped it down, then quickly took a swig of Mum's champagne that Bedaux had poured into granite cups. The champagne fizzed up his nose as he took a big swallow.

"Your turn, pardner," Chris said, turning to Hoot.

Now real food was being served. Canned turkey, roast ham, sausages, sweet potatoes, corn on the cob, pickles, cheese, fresh bread, and a whole table of desserts: pies, cakes, and a plum pudding that the cook set on fire before serving with rum sauce.

Whatever the reason—the champagne, the good food, or the fact that they'd made it to Fort Ware and home was just downriver — Chris was feeling good. He went over to Kati. "How're you doing?" he asked shyly.

"Fine. What about you? You've had quite a few adventures on this trip."

"I guess so."

"I'll never forget being on this expedition," she said, "or this beautiful, savage, wild country of yours."

"Sometimes we who live here forget how great it is." He didn't care if he sounded stupid. He wanted to talk to her, to find out about her life before coming North, how she really felt about the expedition, and what she planned to do when it was all over. So, he asked her.

"I was eighteen on my last birthday, and this trip was a gift from Monsieur Bedaux. He said if I came it would stay in my mind forever. He's right."

Chris thought he'd never seen such beautiful eyes, a hazel colour with flecks of gold.

He knew everyone was watching, including Big John, but the burly policeman was busy eating and didn't seem too excited about Chris talking to Kati, nor did anyone else. He got braver. "Let's go outside," he said, and she nodded.

They walked down to the river's edge. The moon was up, and the air was clean and cold. The horses were happy to have good grazing, and the people were happy for the same reason.

"Tell me about your life in New York," Chris said.

"Madame Fern and I are cousins," she began. "Our mothers are sisters. You have heard of the Lombard family of Grand Rapids, Michigan?"

Chris shook his head.

"They are business people," she said. "Cousin Fern and Uncle Charles — I call him that even though he isn't really my uncle — met in 1916 when he set up The Bedaux Company in Grand Rapids. When this expedition was being planned I didn't know if I should come or not, but it became very important for me to get away."

"Why?" Chris noted how her skin took on a silvery tone in the moonlight. Her thick dark hair curled over her shoulders. She had a nice low voice, the kind a person could listen to for hours.

"I have to make a serious decision," she said. She hesitated, as if wondering whether to say more. Chris figured he must look like the trustworthy type, because she continued. "I have just completed school, a kind of school you don't have here — Miss Finley's Finishing School for Young Ladies."

Chris laughed. "No, there aren't many schools of that type around here, but I know what they are. I was educated in Vancouver, and there are ladies' schools there."

"Oh," she said, as if the idea of a Northern cowboy going to a private city school hadn't occurred to her. "Well, I was afraid to come, at first. But when I thought of the consequences . . . "

"What consequences?"

"I have no money," she said defiantly. "My father made some bad business investments, and when he died we were left with nothing. Monsieur and Madame Bedaux paid for my education. Now, John Porter, the eldest son of my father's former business partner, wants to marry me."

"That sounds okay, but aren't you kind of young?"

"No, it's not okay, and I'm not too young!" Her eyes blazed. "But if I say 'yes' simply because I have nothing else to do, it's not okay at all. I would regret never doing anything on my own, for myself. This expedition has given me a chance to see something completely different. Perhaps there is another sort of life for me."

"What can you do? I mean, to make a living for yourself?"

"I've never thought of it."

"Then you have no choice. You'll have to marry someone who can afford to keep you."

She burst into tears. Chris didn't know what to do, so he stood in silence until she stopped, which happened quickly. He could sense her embarrassment, even in the moonlight, and then defiance.

"Miss Finley's school may not have taught me how to make my own living, but it did teach me how to enhance the living that my husband will provide," she said. "I learned household management, and entertainment etiquette."

Chris looked to the trees on the far side of the river. About 250 miles away lived someone who was already independent, making her own living while she finished high school so she could go to university and become a teacher. Someone who'd learned from an early age how to cook and manage a household, and help run a ranch, too. Someone who might never get the chance to taste caviar and champagne, and probably wouldn't care.

He decided to tell Kati about Jessie.

"I've got a girlfriend," he began.

"Aren't you a bit young?"

"I'm seventeen," he lied, then blushed. "No, I'm not. I'm fifteen. But I can still think about her!"

"You're right," she said, laying her hand gently on Chris's arm. "One is never too young to be in love." Her eyes twinkled.

Chris took her hand and they strolled toward the river's edge.

"Tell me about your girl," Kati said, and so he did.

They reached the horse corral and two of the more curious animals came over to check them out. Kati reached up to stroke one horse's nose. He tossed his head, and she laughed and turned to Chris.

"Jessie's the right girl for you, Chris. I can tell. She knows your way of life. It's important that a man and woman understand each other's history. She'll come back from the city, teach, and you will marry."

"And you will go back to the big city," he said, "and you'll marry this John Porter. And you'll be a very fine wife."

The horse nibbled at Kati's hair. She jumped and pushed his nose back behind the rail.

"Well," Chris said, laughing, as they started back towards the tent, "it's good that we've got our lives, and other people's, all figured out." He stopped and turned to her. "I hope you think of us up here, sometime."

"Oh, I will," she said.

She reached her hand over to touch his, and before Chris knew it his arm was around her waist, and he was kissing her. It was a friendship kiss, but it took all his attention. He never even heard the footsteps.

A big hand yanked Kati away, then grabbed Chris by the shirt collar and belt buckle and pitched him into the White Water River. He went over the bank like he was tied to a rock, and into the ice-cold milky water.

He surfaced to see a hand reach out. He grabbed it. Smoky Sloan hauled him up and Hoot Napoleon rescued his hat. Kati was nowhere to be seen, but Big John Chisholm was still standing like a sentry at the spot where he'd tossed him.

"That cool you off, Romeo?" he asked.

Chris dripped his way back to the camp and sat on a stump to pull off his water-soaked boots, socks, jeans and shirt. Then he went inside to fumble into a dry set of clothes. As he dropped onto his plank-floor bed, he wondered if he should just crawl into his bedroll and call it a night. Nah. He'd better face the music.

The cowboys were still sitting around the fire. Someone handed him a steaming cup of coffee, and Tommy Wilde moved over to give him a place on the rough plank bench. He sipped the coffee, wondering how he was going to deal with this embarrassment.

But the boys weren't interested in his escapades. They were more concerned with the trail ahead. Snowflakes started to fall, lightly at first, but soon increased in size and quantity. By morning all the trails would be knee-deep in white stuff.

Chief Davie could speak French so he and Bedaux became instant friends. Chris caught bits of their conversation, which ranged in topic from world politics to the general economy, to the welfare of the Chief's Sikanni tribe.

The layover gave them a chance to repack all the gear, so when they started again they'd have a spruced-up outfit and clear directions. But feed for the horses was already a major concern. There wasn't any. The horses were increasingly hard to keep together, and became so hungry that some gnawed the bark off poles or jackpine trees.

"If Lamarque doesn't send a message soon, or return in person, I'll send out two men to explore the trails we might follow from here to Telegraph Creek," Bedaux announced.

"The coast is a long ways off," Tommy Wilde said, looking at the big white snowflakes. "Two hundred fifty miles of rough sledding."

"I suggest we go through the Sifton Pass, 60 miles to the north, which would take us over to the Liard watershed," Nick Mayo said. "But it's up to you."

Mayo knew the Sikanni Indians of Fort Ware very well, and spent his time in conversation with them, when not helping to repair rigging or sort supplies for the expedition. His machete was a source of admiration to the men of Fort Ware, especially when Mayo demonstrated its use by expertly cutting everything from brush to cloth. "I'll bet you could give yourself a shave with that blade," Johnny said admiringly.

One day Johnny Pierre took Mayo aside. "I have something to show you." Chris accompanied them to a cabin at the far end of the settlement. Back behind the cabin, tied to a tree, was a young grey pup. It jumped about excitedly when the men approached. "Part wolf, part husky," Johnny said proudly. "Got him on a trade. I'm training him this winter to be my next lead dog."

Mayo bent down and examined the pup, checking its teeth, eyes, feet, breadth of chest, and feel of its fur. "What do you want for it?"

"Not selling. It's going to be a good big dog. Enough wolf to make him brave, enough dog to make him useful." Johnny's eyes travelled to Mayo's machete. Mayo followed his gaze.

"That blade came with me from the West Indies," he said. "It's valuable."

"So's this dog."

By the fourth day of the layover, Bedaux decided that some of the men's jobs were finished and it was time to let them go. Included in this group was Commander Mayo. Chris was especially sorry to see Mayo leave. He'd done his share of work and more. He noticed Mayo and Smoky have a long talk, then shake hands as if agreeing to a deal. Then Nick Mayo did something unexpected: he came over to Chris and shook his hand, too. "Good luck, son," Mayo said. "You're a good trail man. I hope we work together again, someday."

He had his gear packed and ready at the dock, but before hopping into the boat, Mayo strode off through the bush in the direction of Johnny Pierre's cabin. Five minutes later he came back leading the wolf pup. Notably missing from his baggage was the long, heavy, broad-bladed machete.

Mayo was now heading back home to the Wicked River, still dressed in khaki shorts, heavy open shirt, thick wool socks, high boots, and the silk bandanna.

"What'll he be doing next?" Chris asked Smoky.

"He'll find some new adventure." Smoky smiled slyly. "Ever hear the term, Soldier of Fortune? Well, you've just met one."

The boat pushed off, and that's the last Chris saw of Commander Edward "Nick" Mayo.

September 15th, the day they left Fort Ware, was definitely winter in the mountains, clear skies and crystal cold. That's when Floyd Crosby decided it would be a good idea to shoot another wild-west movie scene — starring "The Native Wrangler" Chris Haldane. But his role involved a job no "star" would accept. He was directed to swim across the river with a pack of horses.

TWELVE
HEROES & VILLAINS

Floyd Crosby stated that he knew what he wanted in this river-crossing scene, but relied on the cowboys to set up the horses, which he called "props". The animals were packed with empty boxes so they looked ready for the trail but were not burdened by weight.

One camera would be trained on Chris as he rode Flash into the White Water River. When partway across, he was to drift downstream to where the river made a curve. A second camera was set up to catch his return.

He was about to plunge in when Crosby decided there should be two people in the water, and to act as though they were having a fight.

"Yeah, sure," thought Chris, "Hollywood-style, a cowboy-and-Indian fight — in the middle of a freezing river. Like it happens every day." He wanted to laugh until he heard Bedaux select his "partner" — Billy Turner.

Cheers came from some people on the bank who obviously got a kick out of seeing Billy and Chris go for a dunking in the cold river. Mostly, they were grateful it was the young wranglers and not them.

Billy and Chris removed their underwear — that much less to dry out later — and the wind whipped through their jeans and jackets. A fight was the last thing on their minds, and in this cold any punches would be in slow-motion. Whether planned or not the action started, swift and mean, and when Flash lost his footing over they went. Chris managed to swing his leg over and dismount on the down-stream side, clinging onto the saddle. He stopped thinking about the folks on the bank, or even Billy, and started thinking about how to get across that river the quickest way possible.

With Chris in the lead and Billy following, they trailed the 35 horses toward the far bank. Suddenly Billy's horse seemed to be having trouble. Either the water got deep quicker than he'd figured on or his horse lost his footing, and down he went until only his horse's ears, eyes and nose were above water — and Billy in just as deep. Then the horse flipped over onto its side, side-swiped by a partly waterlogged "deadhead" tree floating a couple of feet below the surface. Billy tried to throw himself clear, but one foot seemed caught in the rigging. He yelled once as the water came swirling up over him and the horse.

Billy was in deep danger. Chris remounted and tried to swim Flash toward Billy. He'd nearly reached him when Billy's horse regained its swimming position and start moving again. But there was no Billy Turner. He must be beneath the horse with his foot caught!

Flash, sensing fear, tried desperately to swim to the far bank to join the other horses but Chris reined him around and managed to get close enough to grab Billy's horse's bridle. Chris saw a foot sticking up, caught in the stirrup! Wrapping his rope around the pommel on Flash's saddle, Chris leapt over onto Billy's horse. It grunted and sunk a bit with the extra weight, but he hung on as the horse plunged ahead.

Laying low, he looped his rope around Billy's leg. Then he grabbed his knife from his belt and started slashing at the leather strap holding the stirrup. When he felt it come loose, he scrambled from Billy's horse onto Flash's back. Billy's horse quickly plunged away, grateful for having rid itself of its load.

But Billy was still upside down, unconscious and under water, at the end of Chris' rope. He had no choice but to tow him out.

Finally Chris felt Flash regain his footing on the rocky river-bottom. He slid out of the saddle into the water, plunging alongside the horse and dragging Billy to shore. He threw the unconscious cowboy onto his stomach with his head lowered, pried open up his mouth and began pumping on him to drain out the water. Billy coughed and retched, and threw up a bucket of river. When his breathing became regular, Chris turned him over.

Slowly, the look of panic in Billy's eyes was replaced by their usual brashness. "Well, Haldane, this'll make some movie," he croaked.

Chris had saved Billy Turner's life, and knew that Billy would never forgive him for it.

The two cowboys sat on the gravel bar, regaining their breath, warming themselves in the fire that Chris had built from driftwood. They could hear the cowboys calling from the far shore, and the 35 packhorses and two saddlehorses crashing through the bush around the downstream bend in the river.

"What happened?" Billy finally asked.

"You got caught. Your rubber boot slipped through the stirrup. I cut you free."

"I owe you."

"You owe me nothing. Just buy yourself some better riding boots."

"Yeah."

They looked along the bank where most of the horses had ended up. Someone was going to have to swim across and bring them back.

"There's one thing I'd like to know," Billy said in an oddly quiet voice.

"What's that?"

"Do you have to be everyone's hero?"

Chris looked away. For some reason he felt guilty, although not sure why.

"Do you gotta have every girl in the world?"

"No, there's only one for me," he said.

"So who is it?" Billy asked, but the cowboys caught up to them and he never did give his answer.

Once they'd made sure the young cowboys were okay, the filmmakers couldn't stop talking about the great "footage" they'd captured on film.

"Chris Haldane and Billy Turner are two fine horsemen," Chris heard Bedaux say proudly. "Did you see how they maneuvered those horses in the river? Right on cue!"

"You're a lucky fellow that Haldane was your river-partner," Smoky said quietly, in an aside to Billy.

Billy nodded, sullenly.

"C'mon," Chris said, grabbing Billy's arm. "Let's get out of these wet clothes. I think Monsieur Bedaux might put on another of his famous feasts!"

The ride to the rendezvous point was slow going, and they averaged just ten miles a day. The cowboys hated to see the horses wading through a foot of snow, then plowing through miles of muskeg. When they stopped to make camp, the men had to shovel snow aside in order to set up the tents.

Bedaux was also aware of the poor condition of the horses. Anyone could see they were tired, gaunt and scruffy, and many had developed limps as a result of cuts, bruises or the dreaded hoof rot. The cowboys would quietly keep the worst ones far back on the trail, then take them into the bush and shoot them so the sound wouldn't be heard by the Dudes.

One day, four packhorses were found so infected that there was no choice but to put them out of their misery. That night, Bedaux counted the horses and flew into a rage. "I thought something was happening," he said, "so I counted the horses last night. And tonight, four are missing! Why are you so stupid as to lose horses on the trail? Corral them, tie them, bell and hobble them, but if any more get lost I'll take it out of your pay, all of you!"

"He doesn't know!" Chris said in amazement.

"And he don't need to," Smoky replied. "We're paid to see this thing to the end."

Chris rode back to the main party to hear Tommy Wilde giving a history lesson to the ladies. "This flat country formed part of the famous Klondikers' overland trail of 1898," he was saying. "We're following in historical footsteps."

At Fox Pass, the snow was eighteen inches deep.

"We're stopping," Bedaux announced. "The horses need a rest. We should soon be meeting Messieurs Lamarque and Stone."

Three days later, Lamarque and Stone rode in to camp. They were given a welcoming cheer. But Lamarque brought strong, and serious, advice. "The low ground of the Sifton Pass is the way to go, but not this late in the season," he announced. "Too much snow."

He and Bedaux then held a long, private, session. Their voices could be heard rising in argument, in both English and French.

Bedaux then signaled for everyone to gather around. "Today, September 25, 1934, I have made the final decision," he said dramatically, as the cameras whirred. "We will be going north over the Sifton Pass, down the Driftpile and Kechika rivers to the Liard; up the Liard to Dease River, up that river through McDame, along Dease Lake, and down the Stikine River to Telegraph Creek."

"Bad news," Smoky commented.

Tommy Wilde agreed. "It's too late in the year to be packing in, especially with tired horses and a bunch of dudes."

Chris was bothered more than ever by a feeling that something serious was going on, and that they were the "dudes" in someone's plan. This trip wasn't being made for fun, or to make movies. He decided to talk it over with Smoky. He felt he could trust the old cowboy. Smoky was a loner, but he, like Mayo, was loyal to his friends. Chris was hoping he could count himself as one of them.

"I want to know what this so-called Sub-Arctic Expedition is really all about," Chris said, as he and Smoky stood on the snowy riverbank. "And all those maps and movies."

Smoky turned to Chris, his eyes squinting in the red sun that was sinking behind the mountains. "What of it? What's it to you, or me? We're getting our money, and then we're getting out."

"But, who might pay for such information?" Chris sputtered.

"Don't know. Don't care," Smoky said. "Now come on. Amoo's been banging on the pail for five minutes. Supper'll be frozen if we don't eat it quick."

The trail turned mean, and grass became even more sparse. Bedaux seemed alarmed, with good reason. He was in a big way responsible for the health and the lives of every person and animal on the expedition. The horses were tired, the men were cranky, and the women were clearly annoyed. The trip wasn't fun anymore, yet no one could leave.

One night Chris overheard Bedaux say to no one in particular, "All over the world I'm considered an 'efficiency expert', but I can't battle nature here."

Chris looked over at Smoky, who shrugged. Since Mayo left he seemed to have lost all interest in the expedition. Smoky Sloan and Nick Mayo both had mysterious pasts. Billy was being taken into the Dude's camp, and the older cowboys had long ago adopted the "do the job and get out" attitude. Chris decided it might indeed be best to take Smoky's advice, but he couldn't stop his mind from churning.

At the Sifton Pass camp, they found the best horse feed they'd seen for a long time, so Bedaux decided to lay over for a few days. Crosby took advantage of the horses' regained energy to stage another movie scene, this one supposedly a comedy featuring a bucking rodeo.

They rigged up a "dummy" bucking bronc using a large dunnage bag with a saddle strapped to it, and suspended by ropes to four trees. With a man shaking each rope, they made the thing "buck" like a bronc. Crosby happily filmed. Shot from the waist up, it looked like the real thing as the cowboys rode, were bucked off, and flew through the air to roll around on the snow-covered ground, whooping and hollering.

Tommy Wilde's part, as the pretend camp cook, was to show up wearing spurs and chaps under a white cook's apron, and a big white chef hat replacing his usual cowboy hat. His script called for him to drawl, "None of you dudes know how to ride!" Then Tommy got on the "horse", endured a few good bucks, cried "Enough!", flew off, and marched away to prepare dinner. In real life Tommy was one of the best bronc riders in the area. Chris decided to ask Tommy his opinion of the expedition.

"Can you tell me why Bedaux wanted to make this trek? Why he'd pay half a million bucks to hire wranglers, packers, land surveyors? Buy horses, top equipment, hire the best film guys in Hollywood, to travel overland through trails only mountain goats would try?"

"Same reason a guy gets on a wild bronc," was Tommy's reply. "To see if he can beat the odds."

"He's supposed to be an efficiency expert," Chris said. "This trip is the least efficient thing I've ever been on!"

"Me too," Tommy said, as he headed back to the movie set for his next scene. "But it's a good job and they don't come along every day for us working cowboys."

THIRTEEN
DROPPING THE DREAMS

"They want you for another movie scene," Kati said. Chris stood up and walked with her and Madame back to the "set".

"How are you feeling after the river incident?" Madame Bedaux asked.

"Fine, thank you."

"That young cowboy, Mr. Turner, was very quick in saving you," she went on. "I hear that he risked his own life."

"Bill Turner should get a medal," Kati added. "Do they have heroism medals in Canada?"

Chris was too stunned to say anything. He could only shrug.

"Perhaps Charles can make inquiries when we return to New York," Madame said. "Such an act of bravery should be rewarded. And how wonderful that Floyd caught it on camera. That was fortunate indeed. I can't wait to see the finished film."

"Bill Turner is an interesting person," Kati said, looking over to Billy who was practising rope tricks on the set. "When I praised his quick thinking in the river he got all red and said 'anyone would have done the same.' I don't think that's true at all, do you, Chris? Not everyone has the stuff inside them to be a hero."

Chris had no problem with Billy being honoured, but he wondered how the story got turned around. When the cowboys heard this version they'd straighten it out pronto, and might even produce the severed stirrup rigging.

⬥

Floyd Crosby's new movie idea was to stage a forest fire. He asked Hoot and Skid to locate two large pine trees standing close together but away from others. "I'll ignite them after dark, and film a fabulous action scene while they burn!" he announced.

"That's crazy! It could get away on us!" Chris fumed.

"You try saying 'no' to these guys," Smoky said. "May as well howl to the moon. Just be prepared."

The cowboys organized a bucket brigade that could go into action at a whistle from Tommy Wilde. It gave everyone some assurance that they, and the forest, wouldn't go up in flames.

Hoot and Skid located the trees, and as soon as darkness fell the horses were packed and moved into place. When the fire was set, pine cones blasted fiery red into the night sky like shooting stars. Floyd and Evan were delighted and shot hundreds of feet of film with two cameras.

Crosby had assigned the starring roles of this scene to Billy and Kati, supposedly two lovers who discovered the fire. Chris watched Kati cheer as Billy bravely fought the flames with his slicker, while the rest of the cowboys milled about as "extras", looking lost and rather silly in the subsequent "stampeding horses" scene. Even Big John applauded their act.

⬥

Bedaux had hired two native guides to take the party through the Sifton Pass: Jack Stone from Telegraph Creek and Joe Poole who lived on the White Water. "Everyone back at Fort Ware is making bets on how many horses and people will survive the trip," Poole said to the cowboys. "They say you'll get snowed in and die."

They travelled north through Sifton Pass to the Driftpile River, following it for several miles, then camped on its banks while the surveyors climbed mountains to take readings for triangulation surveys.

"What do you foresee?" Bedaux asked Stone.

"Very soon, much snow come," he said simply.

Bedaux turned to his group. "*Demain matin, neige profonde!*"

When the ladies had gone to the tents, Jack Stone added more serious details. "No one has ever made it through the winter on their own in this high country. People disappear in deep snow, no food, no help. No one will come to rescue you — they can't get in if you can't get out. Your horses will soon be dead, and so will you."

Bedaux turned to the men. "Do any of you know how to make snowshoes? And travel on them?"

"Sure. Most of us are trappers so we know how to travel in snow," Hoot said. "But for you, uh, Dudes, it'll be impossible. And you gotta know it."

"The horses will get trapped in deep snow and be eaten by wolves," Chris added.

Smoky spoke up. "The ladies will have to return. Send them back now, before it's too late."

"If winter sets in early, you'll be in real trouble in those hills," Lamarque said. Everyone noticed he said "you", not "we".

The cowboys backed him up by voicing agreement. Chris and Billy quietly rejoined the group.

"Telegraph Creek is 200 miles from here," Tommy Wilde said. "The plan to go by small boats from there down the Stikine River to the Pacific Ocean won't work at this time of year. If we make it that far, the river will be frozen. That means a trek on snowshoes of more than 100 miles through wilderness country to the ocean."

"That's right," Lamarque agreed. "Near to impossible, I'd say."

Finally Bedaux held up his hands to get everyone's attention. "I'm a man who likes to do the impossible," he said, "but I won't risk others' lives to realize my goals. If someone wants to go back, say so now. Otherwise, we're going on."

Chris looked around the camp. Everyone was completely trail-worn. The horses were a sorry sight. The weather was getting worse by the day.

Chris took a deep breath, then went over to where Bedaux was talking with Swannell and Phipps. "Mr. Bedaux, there's something you should see," he said. Bedaux followed him back.

"Take a look at this." Chris lifted up a hoof of one of the ponies.

Bedaux turned white. *"Mon Dieux!"*

Chris went to the next horse and held up a similarly sore foot. "And there are more," Chris added, gently setting down the horse's foot.

Bedaux looked around at the faces of the men, and at the horses, and for the first time seemed to notice the condition of his outfit.

"Be at the main tent in fifteen minutes," he said. "I'll be making a further announcement."

When Bedaux gathered everyone together for the second time that day, he made no apology for his change of heart.

"On this day, September 30, 1934, I have made the decision to abandon the Sub-Arctic Expedition," he announced, as Floyd's camera rolled. "We will be turning south immediately."

Chris was chopping wood before supper, as much to get away from the mood of the men as anything, when Bedaux came up to him. "I'd like to talk to you about your plans when this trip is over," he said, sitting down on a log.

"Go home, get outfitted, and head out to my trapline on the Clearwater."

"You get mail very often?"

"Yes, when I go home around Christmas, and again before spring break-up."

"Good. I've got some business in France, and when arrangements have been finalized I'll write to you. I'd like some of you boys to come and work in action scenes in my movies. I'll pay all your expenses, of course. Just bring your saddles and riding outfits."

"Any good horses in France?" Chris asked in a joking voice.

"Oh yes. I took back a couple of good saddlehorses when I was here in 1932, when I packed into the Prophet River country from Fort St. John. One's a steel-dust and the other's a buckskin," he said. "Beautiful animals. You'll get along fine with them. They're Western Canadian horses so they understand English commands." He laughed.

Chris could only imagine what it had cost him to take horses from Fort St. John to France.

"And if we need more horses I'll ship others from here," Bedaux added brightly.

Chris had to smile.

"I'd like you to keep this under your hat," Bedaux said. "I've already talked to a few of the other fellows and they're considering my offer. Billy Turner has confirmed that he's willing to come. But I'll let you know for certain, and send the arrangements by Christmas."

"Sounds good to me."

He was about to leave when Chris thought, "it's now or never," and asked him a question that he'd been working around in his mind.

"What attracts you to this part of the country, Mr. Bedaux? Why are you here?"

Bedaux sat down again. "I love it here, Chris. It's clear and clean. I plan on building a place out in the Sustut River country. You know that area at all?"

"I've never been that far west but I hear it's deep snow country, hard to get in and out in the winter."

"That's true. I'm sending surveyors in next summer to map it and perhaps find better trails through the passes."

"Why are you doing this?"

Bedaux looked away, across to the blue folds of hills to the west. "I want to raise cattle, and horses. If we can't trail the cattle out, maybe I'll build a cannery right there and process the meat. We'll set up a housing development, with families, a school for the kids . . ."

The man's demented, Chris thought. No, he's brilliant. He has seen the country first-hand, and filmed and mapped every inch of the trail from Edmonton to the Sifton Pass. When those fellows surveyed in from the coast, he would know every square mile of the country from the coast across the mountains to the interior, and into the United States.

Later, Chris reported to Tommy Wilde what Bedaux had said. "You know that coastal end of the country," Chris said. "What do you make of Bedaux's plans?"

"He's cuckoo," Tommy replied.

The next day the expedition turned around and started back south, leaving Sifton Pass to camp at Fox Pass among stunted pine and scattered windfall trees. Crosby announced that this was a perfect setting to depict "The Failure of the Expedition". The cowboys were instructed to stagger and stumble along the trail through fallen dead trees, supported by walking sticks and carrying huge packs.

Everyone was tired when they stopped to make one last wilderness camp before reaching Fort Ware. After the horses had been unpacked and turned loose to try to find some grass, Bedaux gathered everyone together.

"I want to thank you for taking part in the expedition," he said. "It's been successful in my eyes, although perhaps not in yours.

"I've worked with some of the most talented cowboys west of the Rio Grande, and you boys are tops," Bedaux continued. "The horses suffered, yes, and about that I feel badly. You had some hardships, too, but luckily no major injuries. You've made a little money during the Depression, and perhaps your families will be a bit better off this winter than they would have been otherwise."

"We will celebrate our last day together in the wilderness by having a toast of rum."

FOURTEEN
DESERTERS CANYON

At Fort Ware, Bedaux spoke privately with the Hudson's Bay factor, Jimmy Ware, then called everyone together. "This is the plan," he said. "The main party will travel down the Finlay River by boats that I've hired. They are captained by experienced river-men, so you may feel confident. The remainder of the party will herd the horses further south to find winter pasture."

Before leaving, Bedaux decided to sell off as many animals as possible. The cowboys set to work branding "BX" on their hooves, which would last about a year.

The Citröen mechanic, Charles Balourdet, was quite concerned about the fate of the horses that had served so faithfully. "Vair 'e going, ze 'orse, for eating?" he plaintively asked.

"If we take them to the Police Meadows, they should be able to winter okay," Smoky said. "That's just below Fort Grahame. I know the area. It's got good grass."

While they packed equipment and supplies, Chris had lots of time to think. So many new opportunities had opened up. Should he go to France? To school in Vancouver? Or stay here, trapping for the winter then finding other wrangling jobs? None, he knew, would ever pay this well.

The day of the sale brought buyers for some of the horses. The next night, Bedaux broke out a few bottles of rum and tried to get everyone singing songs. He belted out "Frère Jacques" and a few popular ballads, but no one was in much of a singing mood. When Chief Davie invited a group to his cabin a half-mile downriver, the party really began.

The chief was 85 years old, and spoke English and French, as well as Sikanni. He and his wife owned a phono-graph, and played some records of good dance tunes. "You must teach the ladies to square dance," the chief announced. A square was formed with four couples; two of the chief's granddaughters partnered with Hoot and Skid, Chris with Madame Chiesa, and Billy with Kati.

Alaman left with your corner girl,
Then do-si-do your own!
Then you all promenade, with your sweet corner
maid
Singing, 'Oh Johnny, Oh Johnny, oh!'

Chris's corner maid was Kati. She smiled and laughed as he swung her, then whirled back to Billy who grabbed her possessively.

At the end of the evening, Mrs. Davie set out fresh bannock, strawberry jam, and tea. "This sure beats caviar and champagne," Smoky said.

On the walk back to camp, Hoot, Skid, Smoky, Billy, and Chris followed behind the Dudes. The Dudes began singing songs in French, which sounded nice. Then Hoot started singing:

I want to be a cowboy's sweetheart,
I want to learn to rope and ride
Over the plains and desert,
West of the Great Divide . . .

Soon everyone joined in until the cowboys' lusty, off-key voices overtook any harmonic attempts by the Dudes. Then Smoky Sloan started imitating wolf howls, and the singing stopped completely.

Billy willingly went ahead to comfort the Dudes and "protect" them from the wolves.

The next day was spent cleaning up. The men shaved, had their hair trimmed, washed and sewed their trail-worn clothes, and bought replacement items at the store.

"The main party will wait here for the boats," Bedaux announced. "The cowboys will start tomorrow to take the horses downriver, and turn them loose a few miles below Fort Grahame on the Police Meadows where there's good grazing."

This meant the men and their mounts, plus sixteen packed horses, would have to cross and re-cross the Finlay River. The other 70 or so head would be driven loose without their nose nets, which meant they'd be wandering off to graze.

On October 8th, the packs and saddles were taken across the river by boat, then the horses were repacked. It was fine weather and good trailing country. The cowboys' feed took a turn for the better, too, because the journey was nearly over and the best of everything was being offered, with no need for rationing.

The plan was to reach Deserters Canyon the evening of the second day, where the Dudes' boats would be waiting. Floyd Crosby wanted to take pictures of the boats going through the canyon — hoping for a spill — and intrigued by the canyon's legends of past desertions and mutiny.

His film of the Dudes' boat going through the canyon was action-packed. While running the chutes they came too close to the big rock, slid around and took on water. The Dudes got a good scare as well as a soaking, but Crosby was excited about the footage he'd captured.

"I have arranged for loads of oats to be delivered back to Fort Grahame to feed the horses through the next two winters," Bedaux announced. "By then they will have found permanent pastures and learned to manage on their own."

"You have to hand it to him," Smoky said admiringly. "It'll cost a bundle to buy and freight oats upriver at that time of year, find storage, and keep two men on the payroll for two years to babysit 94 horses."

The cowboys murmured agreement. Bedaux, for all his strange ways, was a fair dude.

On October 14th, the cowboys removed the horses' shoes and bade them farewell. Then they watched them run off to become part of the legendary wild pony herds of the Rockies.

FIFTEEN

DRIFTING HOME

The boats pulled out of Fort Grahame the morning of October 15th, with the occupants wearing every item of clothing they'd brought, including chaps. The weather had suddenly turned cold. "There's no colder place on earth than riding in an open riverboat in the late fall," Smoky said, as he wrapped a horse blanket around his head. They all followed suit until the boat appeared to be carrying monks rather than cowboys.

Forty miles downriver at Pete Toy's Bar they pulled in to cook some lunch. Pete Toy had come from Cornwall and staked claims here, eventually taking out a fortune in gold from this long bar of the Finlay River. He'd married a Sikanni Indian woman and started a fur trading post, but later met with misfortune and drowned in the Black Canyon of the Omineca River.

"You know, Pete Toy's cache of gold has never been found," Smoky said casually to Chris as they stood watching the river. The fog-shrouded water moved dragon-like as it flowed downstream, guarding its secrets.

"You think there really is a cache?" Chris asked.

"I know it," Smoky replied. He turned to Chris. "I found part of it. And I'll be going back to take it out when I get a grubstake together."

"Thinking of taking in any partners?"

"Who?"

"Maybe when I bring out my furs in the spring, I could throw in some money," Chris said. He kept his eyes on the river, letting the old cowboy think for a minute.

"You serious?" Smoky's eyes squinted through his cigarette smoke.

"I'm serious."

"You're young, and a bit jumpy, but I've noticed you can keep your mouth shut. I got the place mapped. Anything happens to me, it's all written down. Banker in Fort St. John has it in his safe." He said nothing for a minute, then, "Five hundred bucks gets you a one-third partnership."

"Who's the third?" Chris asked.

"I think you know."

"Commander Mayo."

"Right."

"How will he feel about you taking me in?"

"We've discussed it. So, you want in?"

Chris laughed to relieve the tension. "Five hundred dollars is one heck of a lot of money," he said. "Tell you what. I'll write you an IOU. When it's paid, we're partners — in a dream."

"On my word," Smoky said, and they shook hands.

Just above Finlay Forks they encountered the treacherous Finlay Rapids. Everyone walked the shoreline, with only the bowman and driver running the boat through.

They pulled in to the trading post at The Forks, made some purchases, and said hello to Chris's family. The Haldanes had been following the progress of the expedition through "moccasin telegraph", and were up to date on the news.

Chris dropped off his gear, except for what he'd need to go to Hudson's Hope and then hike back. He gave his younger brother and sister each a silk scarf that Bedaux had distributed for souvenirs. Then he ran to the dock to rejoin the crew.

Ten miles down the Peace River they pulled over and camped at the mouth of the Wicked River. They were near Nick's and Smoky's home territory. Nick would be out setting up his trapline for the winter, so he wouldn't be attending the final party. They overnighted at an old sweat lodge built from logs that had a round hole in the floor filled with rocks. Perfect! They built up the fire, hung a tarp over the door, and threw water onto the rocks. Steam puffed and hissed, filling the room, cleaning off five months of trail grime.

Thirty miles later they encountered the silent, and treacherous, Ne Parlez Pas Rapids. Luckily, the water was not too high this time of year and the boatmen made it through with no trouble.

The mountains became less forbidding as the Peace River widened above the portage upstream from the Peace Canyon. There, everyone disembarked, as no boat had ever successfully traversed these rapids. Chris had seen a couple of old sun-bleached wooden hulls washed ashore below the portage, grim reminders of foolish challenges. The men's bodies might be found haunting a back eddy months later, and many miles downstream.

When the boat arrived at the portage, the men stowed their supplies in a nearby cabin. Then they made up backpacks containing bedrolls, clothes and some food, and started on the eighteen-mile walk over the portage trail to Hudson's Hope.

They arrived in town late on the night of October 16, shoulder-sore and trail-weary, but excited to be back.

In the morning, everyone met at the North Star Café. No Jessie. People excitedly asked them about the trip, and the cowboys tried to answer questions as they plowed through plates of ham, eggs, fried potatoes, and just-baked bread.

Finally Smoky innocently asked, "Where's that pretty young girl who used to work here? The Watson girl from the Halfway?"

"Oh, she's at school!" the proprietor, Ted Boynton, said. "Still works here on weekends, but she's busy studying every night."

Chris looked over at Smoky and he winked. Chris couldn't get the stupid grin off his face for the rest of the morning.

The upcoming party was to be a two-day affair, with everyone in the community invited. Festivities would include banquets, dances and an impromptu rodeo. "We're going to throw the biggest party Hudson's Hope has ever seen!" Bedaux had said — and that would be some task.

SIXTEEN

PARTY TIME

The rodeo included a spectacular exhibition of Roman riding by Hoot and Skid. Each man held the reins of two horses while standing with a foot on the back of each, and racing at top speed for a quarter-mile down the dirt road. The Dudes were awestruck by the performance and Bedaux awarded each rider a silver buckle. Then everyone dispersed to get ready for the dinner and dance to follow. When Chris looked for Jessie, she was gone.

Chris arrived in the hotel dining room to see Bedaux mixing rum punch in a big washtub. Amoo was placing a little lemon slice into each glass before he ladled in the drink. Mesdames Fern, Josephine, Bilonha and Kati then passed a glass to everyone as they entered the room.

Next came caviar and toast, to the amazement of the guests who didn't know Bedaux. The cowboys felt like old hands with this kind of food, and made a big show of enjoying it although it still took a bit of acting.

Einar Olson, more grizzled than ever after a season on his gravel bar sluicing gold, looked at his fancy glass of punch held in one gnarled hand, and the bitty piece of toast topped with a wiggling mass of caviar in the other.

"What in tarnation's this?" he demanded.

"That's rum, Einar!" said Smoky, laughing. "Drink 'er down."

"I know rum when I see it, but why'd they have to mess it up by sticking fruit in it? Lemons is for coughs!

"And this stuff here . . . " he lofted his scrap of toast. "This looks like something I use to catch trout! Smells like it, too."

"It'll make your hair grow, Einar. Go ahead." Hoot popped a piece into his own mouth and grinned with pleasure.

"Over the gums onto the tongue — watch out belly here she comes!" Einar cried, and bravely opened his mouth. With no teeth to chew the crusty toast, he had to push it around a bit to soften it, giving the fish eggs lots of time to get his taste buds rolling. His toothless mouth drew up in a little round "o" and his eyes watered, but his Adam's apple bobbed as he bravely swallowed it down. His glass of rum punch followed the caviar in one long swallow.

Then Chris noticed Jessie across the room talking with Kati and Madame Bedaux. She was holding a glass of champagne with her little finger extended, as if she was used to these thin-stemmed things, and balancing her caviar and toast expertly on a dainty serviette. She was the type of person who could be at home anywhere — a country girl at heart but with lots of poise. The thought crossed Chris's mind about how he might ever fit into her life, not the other way around.

Although everyone had dressed up, Tommy Wilde looked spectacular. He wore custom-made boots, a shirt that flashed with hundreds of sequins, tailored frontier pants, silver spurs, and a fringed and beaded jacket made for him by local Indians. As a gift, Bedaux gave him a calfskin duffel bag made by a New York outfitter, Abercrombie and Fitch.

Big John Chisholm, bearded and looking more like a Finlay River trapper than the gamekeeper of a French villa, lead a rousing thank-you toast to Bedaux for organizing and so generously financing the expedition.

Bedaux stood up to respond. "This day, October 19, 1934, will never be forgotten. I have been all over the world but never have I travelled with such a talented and good-natured group.

"While I am disappointed that we did not accomplish our mission to reach Telegraph Creek, I take satisfaction from knowing that we have discovered what I believe is the logical route for an international highway linking the United States, Canada and Alaska. I am going to present a report, together with the data we gathered, to the international highway commission, with the suggestion that the route be considered. The route has been fully mapped by Mr. Swannell, and I firmly believe such a highway will be built. It would lead through the Peace River district, up the Halfway River to Muskwa and Fox Valleys and through Sifton Pass. It would be of great economic value and possibly might play an important part in defence in this continent should the occasion arise. It possesses great scenic value, for it crosses the most fierce mountains of the North yet is quite level.

"Now, let me say one word about the spirit of our party," Becaux continued. "I could never have believed that men would do so much, would risk their very lives time and time again, for the wage of four dollars a day. A spirit grew up among the party where each would try to outdo the other for the good of the whole."

Here laughter and some jeering was heard from the crowd, with eyes turned toward Chris and Billy who grinned sheepishly.

"You men worked, some of you, from four o'clock in the morning until eleven o'clock at night and at times were in actual danger for your lives. Yet you endured every hardship."

Here he paused, as if reluctant to recall the dark side of the trip. "The horses, I admit, were pushed too hard. The constant rain made it impossible to fully dry the saddle blankets and some developed sore backs. We had enough horses but not enough horse strength. The animals became exhausted by their work in the mountains and their struggles with the floods. They were overloaded, too, as we pushed through the Muskwa Pass, which I understand has been renamed by the geographer as Bedaux Pass. You will recall the terrible weather we endured, and how it took us five days to accomplish 65 miles from the top of the Rockies to White Water, fording eight streams swollen from incessant rains. The horses . . . "

Bedaux hesitated once again. Chris glanced over to see how Jessie was taking this news, which he hadn't related in his letters. Her eyes were downcast, staring at the table in front of her. He noticed the disturbed looks of the women from the expedition as they were made aware of the hardships that had been shielded from them, as much as possible, on the trip.

"The horses suffered, very much. The food was scanty and they continually strayed from camp to find fodder. One night we did something cruel. We kept the horses tied all night without food, but we knew we would need them the next day and couldn't afford to have them get away.

In the morning we awakened to find eight inches of snow on the ground and it was still snowing hard. But we pushed ahead, in the midst of the storm. As we made camp that night I became aware, clearly, for the first time, of the horses suffering from hoof rot. And all were exhausted. Still the snow fell, to a depth of eighteen inches. One night we had to shoot three horses, just taking them off the trail, and the next morning five more were incapacitated from exhaustion. We left them to the wolves. Near the end, out of 130 horses only 90 or so were fit for loading. It was no longer safe or sane to go ahead. The expedition was at its end."

Monsieur Bedaux stared ahead, past the people, out through the window of the hotel and into the dark starry night. He cleared his throat. "I hope to see you all again, and so I shall not say 'good-bye', but *au revoir* — until we meet again."

The banquet was excellent: roast beef, chicken, garden vegetables, potatoes, pickles, salads, and bread and buns, topped off with homemade ice cream and apple pie.

"This sure beats our trail meals," Smoky said.

"Hey, no insults to the cook!" called Amoo, who'd over-heard.

"We're sure going to miss your tasty trail stew," Chris called out.

But the best thing for Chris was Jessie being there. He hadn't had a chance to even say hello to her until the banquet began. Then, when the moment came, he suddenly became shy. *What if she's forgotten me?* he thought. *What if she's decided that Billy Turner is a better deal? After all, he owns a ranch with his dad, while I have nothing.* Chris had seen her talking to Billy and touching her fingers gently to his swollen nose. Chris winced, even if Billy didn't.

While the tables were being cleared, Bedaux got down to business. He sat at a table in the corner and invited the crew, one at a time, to come to have a private talk with him.

Bedaux started his talk with Chris by again complimenting him on the way he handled horses. "You remember my offer to work in the movies, on location in France?"

Chris nodded. He looked around the room at the faces of people who'd been friends all his life, and some who he'd come to know on the expedition. Billy, his face bruised and with one black eye, was busy charming Madame Fern and Kati with some wild story. Billy chanced at that moment to look over at Chris, and gave a lopsided grin. Although the two would likely never become friends, Chris knew he'd be going down the river with Billy again, and that was okay. He could handle a dozen Billys if he had to.

"I will be making arrangements for Mr. Turner to come to France," Bedaux said, following his glance. "He will make a perfect villain for the silver screen, don't you think so?"

Chris looked at Bedaux, surprised. "Then you knew about him, and me, and the scene in the river?"

Bedaux smiled.

"I'm not sure what I'll do," Chris finally answered. "I'll have to think it over."

"I'll let you know by Christmas if the job is a go-ahead."

"I'll look for your letter," Chris said. He stood up and offered his hand. "Thank you, Mr. Bedaux. Getting hired on this expedition changed my life."

Bedaux looked at Chris strangely. "I always wonder, when I come into a new area, if the disturbance my presence creates is good, or bad," he mused.

When the music started at the schoolhouse, Chris held out his hand and he and Jessie moved onto the dance floor. They whirled around the room, moving in rhythm with one another. "I've never felt so comfortable with anyone in my life," Chris marvelled to himself.

Billy Turner danced past with Kati. He grinned over at Chris, which surprised Jessie.

"I have so much to tell you," he said in answer to her quizzical look.

"Good," she said. "I've got time to listen."

The dance went on until early morning. Then more food was laid out.

"We've gotta be up early to go back to Fort St. John," Tommy Wilde said. "You coming downriver with us for the next party, Chris?"

"No, this is where our trails part," he replied. "I have a promise to keep."

He looked over at Jessie and smiled, but this promise was not to her. It was to himself, to make the pilgrimage to the Two Mountains That Sit Together.

The morning of October 20th dawned cold and drizzling with rain. The ride downriver in open boats didn't look like much fun, with only a few pack mantles to keep off the rain. The Dudes' boat had a sort of tent stretched over the top, but even that wouldn't keep them dry and it sure wouldn't be very warm.

A dozen or so local people stood at the landing to say good-bye to the Fort St. John cowboys and to the Dudes. Billy Turner was travelling by boat as far as the Halfway. From there, he would walk the 60 miles to his ranch. Skid and Hoot were getting their outfits ready for a winter on the trapline. Smoky was staying a few more days in Hudson's Hope to outfit himself before he returned up the Peace River to his home territory on the Wicked River.

Kati and Billy Turner were standing by the dock talking intently. Their hands touched, then dropped, and Billy stepped away. Chris decided now was the time to say his own farewell to Kati. He went up and held out his hand in a formal way. She shook it, smiling.

He looked over at Billy, who was watching closely. "I guess you and Billy might be staying in touch," he said.

"Perhaps. He wants to come to France next spring when Uncle Charles can make arrangements. He will be reporting to Mr. Chisholm at the Bedaux estate at Candé . . . and I think I might be in Paris next winter, also."

"If you don't get captured by your New York businessman first!" Chris joked.

A serious look crossed her face. "I don't think that will happen. On this expedition I met independent people like you, and Bill, who are so brave! You aren't afraid to try new things. And Jessie, she plans to become a teacher. How exciting! So, I've learned things from all of you!"

She kissed Chris lightly. Billy quickly moved ahead to help her into the boat.

The Hudson's Hope group stood waving as the boats chugged into the main channel. Then the engines roared into action, the boats rounded the bend in the river, and were gone.

SEVENTEEN
MESSAGE FROM THE MOUNTAINS

The rain had turned to a fine mist by the time Chris left Hudson's Hope to walk twenty miles to Moberly Lake. It was easy to follow Maurice Creek and then an old survey cut-line. The windfall trees that blocked the trail were more of a nuisance than an obstacle.

"Good grass here," Chris noted. This was a favourite area for the Indians to hunt. They could turn their horses loose here to winter, and in the spring they'd be in good shape.

He arrived at the west end of Moberly Lake, and was told by old Mrs. Dokkie that most of the people were out in the bush, preparing their winter's meat. He decided to walk five miles further to where they often camped.

He was greeted warmly, but with sad news. "Chief Dokkie and his band were taken to police court last week for trespassing on a trapline. They said it now belongs to a white man — but it's on our traditional hunting grounds!"

Not too long ago, the Indians never had to register their traplines. With white people coming into the area, the government had made it a law that all traplines, whether used by Indians or whites, must be registered. It had caused no end of problems, but the government had warned that if steps weren't taken now, worse problems would result.

Harry Garbitt, who ran the trading post in Moberly, had interpreted and the chief got off with a suspended sentence.

"The Indian Agent, Dr. Brown, is trying to buy back some of our trapping areas for us, but he's not having much luck," John Desjarlais said. "There's going to be war out in the bush some day."

Chris stayed for a meal, but one meal led to another, and when it was learned that he planned to stay on the twin peaks, the legends came to life. After a dinner of roast moose and bannock, everyone sat around the fire, watching the flames cast eerie shadows. Then Mrs. Desjarlais was ceremoniously brought out to the campfire and settled warmly onto a blanket.

"She has a story to tell," said John Dokkie. "It's about the mountains. She was a young girl when her people left Manitoba. She was on the journey to come here."

Chris squatted on his heels to hear once again the legend of the trek that had brought the Saulteaux Indians from the Red River area of Manitoba west to British Columbia, to share the Moberly lakeshore with the Cree and the Beaver tribes.

Following the Red River conflicts in Manitoba in 1870 and the Northwest Rebellion in 1885 in Saskatchewan, there had come a time of tension, with the fear of further uprisings. The Saulteaux people were starving. The buffalo had been extinguished and this animal was the centre of their lives. White settlers were taking over the lands the Indians had freely roamed upon. In hunger, their hunters killed four cows belonging to a settler. They knew there would be trouble and so, afraid of reprisal and in search of a better life, eight families travelled west into Alberta to the Rocky Mountains.

Mrs. Desjarlais now related, first-hand, the story of how the band had followed their leader, Ka-Ka-Koo-Ka-Nis, whose name means Raven Bone in English.

"Early on the journey Raven Bone went to sleep and visited the Spirit Land to learn what he should do," she began. "He rode his black stallion into the bush. Neither he nor the stallion ate for four days. He had a vision, and came back to tell the people what he saw. 'We must hide in a deep valley on the prairie because the red-coats — the North-West Mounted Police — will be coming for us. Make sure the kids are full.'

"So we made a fire to cook because we would not be able to make a fire when we were hiding. Dogs, horses, everyone, ate and had drinks. Then we tied the mouths of dogs and horses, and we kids were told not to cry. We stayed up all night holding the animals, because there was no place to tie them." Mrs. Desjarlais's eyes stared into the embers of the fire, remembering that time so long ago.

"In the morning, there was a mist covering everything. We could hear the hooves coming. We could not see the horses, but no one could see us, either. When the sun came up, the mist went away. We thought Raven Bone had made the mist for us."

"That's when you came to Rocky Mountain House and further to Lac Ste. Anne, travelling North," someone prompted.

"Yes. Raven Bone said, 'You have to leave me. I will talk to my powers.' He went away with the stallion for two nights. We waited for him three miles away, and made no noise. Then Raven Bone called all of us, even the children, and told what he had seen: a woman lying flat on her back, her breasts standing up and so full of milk that she was feeding all of us.

"We kids didn't say anything but the adults said, 'What does this mean?' Raven Bone said, 'These are mountains, north-west from here. If we go, the plenty of the mountains will forever protect and feed us.'"

Chris knew that they had journeyed through the Monkman Pass to the Wolverine Mountains, north down the Parsnip River and over to the twin mountains that lay to the west of a lake that lay west and east, exactly like the vision seen by Raven Bone. They had stayed one winter, and there had met the Beaver Indians.

"When Raven Bone went into the mountains, he slept for three days," Mrs. Desjarlais went on. "He didn't breathe and his heart stopped, but the pulse in his neck still pumped with life. When he awoke, the people recognized that he would be the prophet of our tribe until the Creator decides its time for a new one.

"He told the people that he had seen visions of the world ending. From that time, the Two Mountains That Sit Together were known to be sacred, and he was acclaimed as a prophet.

"Ka-Ka-Koo-Ka-Nis was not supposed to be buried, but he was anyway, on the twin mountains," Mrs. Desjarlais continued. "The mountain sheep circled his grave until their path was worn deep in a ring. The people were afraid because of their error, and exhumed the grave. But nothing was there. Nothing was inside the grave."

Chris knew that some Crees later joined the Saulteaux as treaty Indians to share the east end of Moberly Lake, while Beaver bands occupied the west end of the lake, as well as areas on the upper Peace and on the Halfway rivers. Trails from all the tribes and bands came together along rivers and through valleys to what had been named in Cree as *Kanesostegaw Asineewachia*, The Two Mountains That Sit Together. The various local tribes had continued to share this place for ceremonies or for hunting.

The fire had died down; it was time to sleep.

The next morning Chris started his trek toward the mountains. Perhaps the spirits would bring him the same strength as they had others. He was prepared for this visit. The Moberly Lake people had given him a kind of natural tobacco called *o'chukasimina*, made from small red ground berries that the partridges eat. He would give this as an offering. He also had some inner bark of red willow, and *wehkimasikan*, a fungus that grows on diamond willows, to burn, which would purify his thoughts.

The trail narrowed, and it became difficult to see anything but the mountains. Tall thick poplars and tamarack cut his view to right and left, but the mountains rose high and stately, outlined against the cold blue sky.

Two posts had once guarded the mountains, with pictographs showing the boundaries of the Cree/Saulteaux and Beaver territories. Once, on the trail coming from the west toward the mountains, his grandmother had shown him other pictographs on a rock cliff near Silver Sands. He remembered them being like a map, red in colour, and high up. There were more paintings found north of Carbon Creek.

Chris knew he would soon come to the fast-flowing creek where he would find the cross, or medicine pole.

That is where he would make his offerings, and sing the sacred songs he'd been taught long ago.

His grandmother had told him that 200 years ago a Beaver prophet dreamed that there would be white people coming here who would build a big path through the bush, using loud machines. "Never!" Chris thought as he threw down his pack beneath a spruce tree. He walked, unencumbered, to a cross which represented the four sacred directions. Two eagles screamed above. He heard a rustle in the bush, and a deer flashed away. Slowly he circled the cross, singing. His voice echoed until it sounded like many.

He circled four times, when he suddenly felt tired. The singing sounds rose and fell, making him feel dizzy. He stumbled to the spruce tree, spread out his bedroll and fell asleep, his head to the east. The wind pushed aside the branches of the tree, letting in flashes of light. The boughs whistled and sighed and whispered in strange tongues. Chris lay, unmoving, neither sleeping nor awake, absorbing the message from the mountains.

The trees around him slowly turned from green to black, but it was not because of night. The poplars and willows bent, and their leaves shrivelled. Water from the fast creek slowed, became thick and black like the oil he had seen leaking from the wrecked Citröen cars. This black sludge surged down the creek beds, foaming purple, to be sucked into caves and disappear. The ground was dry, the grass sparse and brittle.

"If white men harm the rivers this earth will die." The words seemed neither spoken nor written, just there. "If people learn the natural way of life, the earth will survive.

"But when men drill holes into mountains, the creeks will become black, the fish will be dead. When men block the beds of rivers, water will drown the land. The valley will become like an ocean. The animals will drown. There will be no sheep in the Clearwater River. People's homes will be gone forever."

Chris heard himself cry to the Spirits, "Show me the way to help! Provide a path!" but the voices continued to whisper their messages of doom, mocking his cries, and the tree branches moaned and twisted in the wind.

"Take the message to the people!" The voices became louder, urgent. "Tell the story! *Eyimewahtik ka tahkonaman!* Carry the cross!"

He put his hands to his face, and found it wet with perspiration. He threw back the blanket and stumbled away from the protection of the trees to stand on the rocks, arms out, his body still as the cross.

Night fell once again. Two days and two nights passed. Then the sky became clear, and the stars and moon shone over snow-covered peaks. Chris knelt to drink at the creek, but the water looked dark and slow-moving, like syrup, and he stood up, afraid of being poisoned.

"Tansisi eyimewahtik ka tahkonaman? How can I carry the cross?" His voice did not echo, but stopped dead, the wind throwing it back at him, taking away his power to be heard. He sat down and felt the cold damp ground penetrate his clothes.

Chris thought of where he'd been, the country he'd seen, the people he'd come to know. They had seen value in this land, but they saw different riches. Bedaux had talked of the freedom the people had here. And how other people would someday want this freedom, this clean air and water, and the vast land with its valuable minerals, and timber. But where did lovers of the land fit into this new age?

Above, in the tree, sat an owl. It puffed its throat to answer the call of another. A wolf's howl joined their sound, and another, until the surrounding hills echoed eerie scales: up, down, loud, soft, hollow, haunting.

Chris crawled back into his bed, his head aching as if he'd been hit by a hammer.

In the old days, young people were sent to the mountains for a minimum of four days to see which good spirit might take pity on them. This spirit would be their advisor. The gifted ones would get more than one, adding to their knowledge as they got older, if they had a good heart.

But some went wild, and stayed to live forever with the animals. Only the medicine people could bring them back, by singing the good songs and giving them the right foods and medicines. Chris had been on the mountain four nights. Might he choose to remain forever with the wolves and bears? He wanted to. He lay, his thoughts tangled.

This land and its wildlife must be cared for. It must have a Keeper. But who?

Perhaps himself. He must choose, now — to become one of the wild ones and stay, never to be seen again by human kind. Or, to come down from the mountains with greater knowledge.

He'd had a vision of what could happen if their sacredness was forgotten.

He got to his feet, opened his arms, threw back his head.

"*Pako kwayas ka eyimewahtik ka tahkonaman!*" Chris cried. "I will carry the cross! And I will carry it well."

EPILOGUE
MYSTERIES OF THE DEAD

When rumours began to circulate that Commander Edward Mayo, the former British Naval officer, had been paid by the British Secret Service to report on the Bedaux Sub-Arctic Expedition, Chris didn't believe it. But he had to believe the next news he heard about Mayo. In November 1936, two years after the expedition, a Vancouver newspaper announced his fate.

BANDITS SLAY TWO B.C. MEN
MAJOR J.C. HARTLEY AND
COMMANDER EDWARD MAYO GEAKE
MURDERED IN MEXICO.

The men were ambushed in Durango State by Mexican banditos while supposedly seeking a lost gold mine.

Smoky Sloan also disappeared from the Peace country, never to be seen again. And so Chris Haldane became sole owner of the legendary lost gold of Pete Toy's Bar.

Charles E. Bedaux's fate was announced in newspaper headlines, in January 1943.

BEDAUX, MYSTERY MAN,
FACING TREASON CHARGES,
KILLS SELF

The Bedaux Sub-Arctic Expedition brought together a unique collection of people, and animals, to perform an impossible task. Today, the reason for the expedition remains an unsolved mystery.

Chris Haldane became aware, that day on the mountains, that he had been chosen to receive special knowledge. Today, the Two Mountains That Sit Together (sometimes called Twin Sisters or Beattie Peaks) overlook a vast, 640-square mile, hydro-electric dam reservoir instead of the network of rivers, and the Peace River valley lies buried beneath 600 feet of water. But the twin mountains still rise majestically, awaiting the next Keeper of the Sacred Medicine Cross.

Printed in April 2000 by

VEILLEUX
ON DEMAND PRINTING INC.

in Longueuil, Quebec